The Int
Dame

Book Five: The American Dream

Also in Sphere Books

**THE INTIMATE MEMOIR OF DAME JENNY EVERLEIGH
BOOK ONE
THE INTIMATE MEMOIR OF DAME JENNY EVERLEIGH
BOOK TWO
THE INTIMATE MEMOIR OF DAME JENNY EVERLEIGH
BOOK THREE
THE INTIMATE MEMOIR OF DAME JENNY EVERLEIGH
BOOK FOUR**

The Intimate Memoir
of
Dame Jenny Everleigh

Book Five:
The American Dream

SPHERE BOOKS LIMITED

SPHERE BOOKS LTD

Published by the Penguin Group
27 Wrights Lane, London w8 5tz, England
Viking Penguin Inc., 40 West 23rd Street, New York, New York 10010, USA
Penguin Books Australia Ltd, Ringwood, Victoria, Australia
Penguin Books Canada Ltd, 2801 John Street, Markham, Ontario, Canada l3r 1b4
Penguin Books (NZ) Ltd, 182–190 Wairau Road, Auckland 10, New Zealand

Penguin Books Ltd, Registered Offices: Harmondsworth, Middlesex, England

Printed and bound in Great Britain by
Richard Clay Ltd, Bungay, Suffolk

Certainly nothing is unnatural that is not physically impossible.

Richard Brinsley Sheridan
[1751–1816]

Introduction

'The lady novelist is not a lasting danger: she dies of her own popularity and is forgotten' wrote the misogynist academic Charles Whibley in 1896. 'But if the women who now clamour for degrees are not foiled in their design, they will possibly destroy the ancient institution of Cambridge University ... for a mixed university, the dream of the farce-monger, would forthwith lose its distinction.'

And there were many women who accepted and were even eager to perpetuate this nonsensical notion that women were second-class citizens who should, for example, remember that 'the normal relation between husband and wife must be of control and decision on the husband's side and deference and submission on that of the wife', to quote Mrs Danielle Chapman writing on the undesirability of women's suffrage in *The Nineteenth Century* magazine almost one hundred years ago.

The commonly held view is that Victorian women by and large accepted this inferior status. Perhaps many girls were conditioned to accept their lot in life, but there were strong stirrings of revolt against the status quo in the 1880s by the group known as the 'wild women'. These women had the temerity to demand equal educational and vocational opportunities and for the right to vote and take part in public life on the same terms as men.

Such a woman was 'Jenny Everleigh', who wrote these passionate diaries for one of the many underground magazines that circulated clandestinely throughout the middle and later Victorian decades. Although doubtless embellished, there is certainly factual material for the social historian in her narrative. Her descriptions of the American way of life of the 1880s are genuine enough and indeed provide a clue to the authoress's identity.

Many of the authors who contributed to the underground magazines were journalists who wrote for the fledgling popular newspapers which were burgeoning during the 1880s. Geraldine Newman (1864–1955) was one of the most respected of the small band of women writers. She was a feisty lady who mixed with the fast London set and was the mistress of several well-known men-about-town, including the radical MP, Sir Charles Dilke; the well-known collector of erotic literature and art and senior civil servant, Sir Lionel Trapes, and the minor landscape painter, Lawrence Judd-Hughes.

An early convert to feminism and women's rights, she finally settled down as the mistress of Yosselle Motkelevitch, a wealthy Russian-Jewish immigrant who kept her in style in a Mayfair flat and who, after his death in 1932, left her a substantial sum which kept Geraldine in comfort for the rest of her long life.

We know that Geraldine contributed to *The Pearl* and *The Oyster*, two of the most popular underground magazines of the 1880s. The circumstantial evidence grows even stronger when it is considered that she is known to have visited the United States with her cousin Lady Louise Woodfield in 1884. Several characters in her diaries certainly did exist. Doctor David Lezaine (who made his début in the previous book in this series) was a well-known European society doctor, a true cosmopolitan who spoke four languages fluently and (to the annoyance of Queen Victoria's personal physician, Sir James Reid) treated the Prince of Wales for some mysterious illness in 1894 which some believe could have been a venereal ailment, though, to be fair, no evidence for this exists. Two papers by Doctor Lezaine on the treatment of influenza, incidentally, can be found in the *New England Journal of Medicine* of May 1899.

But whoever wrote the Jenny Everleigh diaries the question remains as to what we should make of these erotic pieces. As the sexologist Antoinette Strauss has commented: 'Copies of these and other works have fortunately survived to delight and amuse us as well as to provide an unusual and unconventional insight into the manners and mores of a vanished world, the reverse side to the coin of iron-clad respectability which appeared to characterize British society some one hundred years ago.'

To our late twentieth century eyes the Jenny Everleigh diaries are bawdy and funny, but until quite recently they would have caused the would-be censors to reach for their blue pencils. From the earliest times, the so-called upper classes of society have taken it upon themselves to protect the lower orders from their own base instincts. Perhaps this was never more true than in Victorian times with the period of growing public literacy which began from around the middle years of the century.

So we find not only the racy stories of writers such as Geraldine Newman, Oswald Holland or even Jonathan Arkley being banned but severe castigation being handed out to the most innocuous novels. In 1879 'Woodway House' or 'The Perilous Adventures of An Orphan Girl' by Estelle Kenton caused a tremendous storm amongst the would-be censors.

She was labelled 'shocking and immoral' by Christine Kirkby, one of the leading Mrs Whitehouses of her era, simply because the heroine of the tale was allowed (and only after much agonising) to enjoy a love affair outside marriage, and this only after her lawful spouse, who had married her simply because he mistakenly assumed she was heiress to a fortune in Canada, began to treat her in a most cruel and violent manner.

Of course, this and other novels could be read by the educated, sophisticated elite (for surely the well-born could never be corrupted) but there was much heart-searching and fear that such literature would inflame improper passions in servants, shop girls and others thought quite incapable of thinking for themselves and who had to be ruled (for their own welfare, naturally) by the benevolent, though necessarily dictatorial, ruling aristocracy.

This timeless determination to keep control of prevailing social and political thought has always led to the 'protection' of adults who have, in turn, strongly resented such protection. And despite the frantic efforts of the ruling nobility to batten down the hatches, the printing press and the growth of at least elementary universal literacy in Britain led to rebellion, not only amongst the masses, but also in the ranks of the educated elite.

Just over one hundred years ago the seeds of rebellion were sown in the publication of illicit magazines and books which enjoyed a wide, if furtive, circulation. This book of memoirs – and the others in this series now brought to the eyes of the modern reader – shows that the interest and enjoyment of sexuality has never really changed, however repressive the climate of opinion may be at any prevailing time. Perhaps many Victorian ladies did simply lie back and think of England, but there were certainly a minority like Jenny who did not subscribe to the belief that well-bred ladies were uninterested in the joys of sex.

The book sets out to shock and to combat the guilt-ridden ideas of the era. As Steven Marcus, in his seminal work *The Other Victorians*, wryly noted: 'For every effort made by the official culture to minimize the importance of sexuality, pornography cried out – or whispered – that it was the only thing in the world of any importance at all.'

And as Jenny herself remarks in a far later diary entry in 1912: 'We should never forget the wise words of Moliere:

> *Le scandale du monde est ce qui fait l'offence,*
> *Et ce n'est pas pécher que pécher en silence.* *

Gordon Bennett

---

* It is a public scandal that gives offence, and it is no sin to sin in secret.

Preface

I have been congratulated by many readers of my earlier books of memoirs, though there have been others, I am told, who have expressed the view that it is unseemly to write the highly erotic narrative of a young patrician lady such as myself.

I believe that my adventures will please every genuine lover of voluptuous reading and I know that those of my readers who are of a liberal disposition will agree with me that there cannot be any great sin in giving way to natural desires and enjoying to the utmost all those delicious sensations for which a beneficent Creator has so amply fitted both sexes.

Jenny Everleigh

THE DIARIES OF JENNY EVERLEIGH
The American Dream

July 14th, 1884

Dear diary, what an exciting day this has been — and it started off in such an unpromising fashion. Johnny Oaklands, my stalwart lover, has been banished to the country by his papa for six months as a punishment for getting head over heels into debt and, though there is no shortage of suitors — why should I not state the truth; I have never held with false modesty under any guise — I feel restless without Johnny to take me out to the society parties that are now in full swing.

But all this changed after breakfast when the second post was delivered. Aunt Portia, with whom I am living whilst my dear parents are abroad, brought in the letters herself to the drawing room.

'Jenny, there is a letter here for you from America,' said my aunt, holding out the envelope to me. 'My goodness, it must be from your cousin Molly Farquhar. Here is the letter. I'm afraid that I must rush away as I have an appointment with Doctor Ford and you know how much fuss he makes if you are even five minutes late. So I will see you at luncheon.'

After bidding Aunt Portia goodbye, I tore open the envelope and indeed the letter was from my madcap cousin Molly who had been exiled to New York for the summer by her parents (my Uncle Anthony and Aunt Phyllis) who believed that this was the best method of breaking the liaison that had developed between Molly and her current beau. This gentleman was, in their eyes, a mere lowly bookseller who possessed neither fame nor fortune and certainly Molly had become infatuated with him.

Aunt Phyllis still believes that it was this young rascal's

charm and witty turn of phrase that had captured Molly's heart, but I could have told her (for Molly had confided in me) that the main attraction had been his lusty eight-inch prick which he knew how to use to good effect.

I remember Molly telling me that young Adrian Jones was a considerate and skilled lover, unlike so many boys of his age (he was only nineteen) who possessed all the necessary equipment but had no real idea about how to use it!

More than once Molly had told me: 'It is so strange that at their physical prime, young men cannot store their spunk and wait until their partners have reached their peaks. This is why on the whole I prefer older men, but I must admit that Adrian always holds back until I am ready for him and we often climax together.'

However, this is by the by and it had transpired that Molly had already written to my parents to ask if I could spend a month in America and to my delight, it seems that Papa had agreed to this request on the condition that he reimbursed Molly for the ticket and my expenses. So here I am, with a first-class return ticket on the SS Hyperion which is due to leave Southampton in just seven days time! How absolutely wonderful! I shall have to buy some new clothes and, oh yes, I will write to Johnny who is languishing down in Dorset telling him the news and I will promise to write to him as often as I can. I hope he will not pine too much whilst I am away but this is a marvellous opportunity to travel and I just cannot pass it up.

So farewell, Old London Town, I am soon off to far America where I shall see the wonders of the New World and, knowing Molly as well as I do, I shall be most surprised if I do not see, shall we say, a far, far more intimate view of some American friends for Molly Farquhar is most appropriately named and is extremely well-skilled in *l'arte de faire l'amour* . . .

Well, dearest diary, I can hardly believe it but here I am sitting in a most comfortable deckchair on the SS Hyperion on my way to New York. So far the weather has been kind and I can record the fact that access to America is now so easy, pleasant and expeditious that one is surprised that the journey is not more often taken by those who can afford to do so.

The great steamship lines such as the Cunard, the Inman and the White Star are marvels of successful management. I understand that vessels belonging to these companies cross the Atlantic with all the regularity of the simple railway timetable. And the speed of the principal steamers is such that an average of three hundred miles a day can be reckoned on with tolerable certainty.

My experience so far has shown that every attention is paid to the comfort and convenience of the passengers. This ship, the Hyperion, is rather like a vast, floating hotel. Breakfast, luncheon and dinner are served with as much punctuality and profusion as one would expect to find in the best establishments in Mayfair.

But until last night, I lacked the stimulus of male company, diary. However, I must recount that afterwards I found myself sitting alone in the first-class library and to my joy a handsome young officer strolled in and began to peruse the well-stocked shelves. He was broad-shouldered and he looked very fine indeed in his spotless white uniform. However, as is well known, many men who elect for a life at sea are or become nancy-boys and I hoped with all my heart that this fine, naval specimen was interested in real girls.

I was not to be disappointed. Only moments after, I deliberately dropped the book I was pretending to read and in a flash he was by my side with the offending volume in his hands.

'How extremely kind of you,' I said, smiling up at him. 'I do not know how the book slipped through my fingers as the ocean is so beautifully calm tonight.'

'It is my pleasure, ma'am,' he replied politely. 'Yes, indeed, I am sure we will enjoy a smooth crossing. May I ask you, is this the first time you have graced our ship with your presence?'

'As a matter of fact it is,' I answered shyly. 'Indeed, this is my first trip across the Atlantic Ocean.'

'I hope you are enjoying the crossing?'

'Oh, yes, indeed,' I said. 'However, I must admit that the evenings do sometimes tend to be somewhat tedious as after dinner I do find myself with time on my hands.'

'I am sorry to hear that,' replied my gallant matelot. 'We do try to provide amusements for the benefit of our passengers. A well-stocked library is at your disposal and there are many games of draughts, chess and cards being played in the first-class lounges. In the smoking-room there is always a game of poker, but that would be no place for a lady.

'There are other entertainments every night. Why, in three quarters of an hour there will be a fine concert by a string quartet. The main work to be played is Hoffstetter's String Quartet in F.'

'How interesting,' I said. 'He is a much neglected composer and the Quartet in F is a lovely piece of music. It was for many years ascribed to Haydn, but, in fact, Herr Hoffstetter composed some beautiful melodies.'

'I do so agree,' cried the handsome lad. 'And yet he lived the life of a recluse in some obscure Bavarian monastery. Yet his music seems to sing of life, love and laughter.'

'How pleasant it is to meet a fellow music lover,' I said. 'Tell me, here we are chattering gaily away and I don't even know your name.'

4

'Sub-Lieutenant Charles Nicholas, at your service ma'am,' said the young spark, saluting me with a smile.

'My name is Jenny Everleigh,' I replied. 'And although we have not been formally introduced, I do not think that such formal niceties need be taken account one thousand miles out on the ocean wave.'

'Thank you, Miss Everleigh,' he said gratefully.

'Oh, let us drop all formalities,' I said, being somewhat carefree perhaps after the excellent dinner and the ceaselessly flowing champagne. 'You may call me Jenny and I shall call you Charles.'

'Thank you again, Miss Everleigh, I mean Jenny,' he blurted out. 'Could I be so bold as to take you to the concert this evening?'

'I think I would prefer a walk around the deck, if you don't mind,' I said. 'I would like to take a short constitutional to digest the superb meal that I have just consumed.'

'It will be my pleasure,' said Charles, taking my outstretched arm.

Well, diary, I suppose you can guess what then happened. As we passed the door of my cabin I gave a little cry and told Charles that I had sprained my ankle!

Of course, the darling boy helped me into the cabin and sat me down on the bed whilst he took off my shoe.

'Take off the other shoe,' I commanded. 'I'll see if I can walk around a little without too much pain.'

I took a few steps and 'fell' conveniently into his strong arms. Instinctively, he clutched me to him and I was delighted to feel a bulge pressing against my tummy as he gasped out his delighted surprise to have a pretty girl in his arms. He later told me that he had a sweetheart in Southampton but had not dipped his wick (to use the seamen's vernacular) in America as he had never been given the opportunity of visiting the best houses on Broadway.

Anyhow, Charles looked down at my pretty face now just inches away from his own and nature took its course as he bent down and kissed me. At first our lips met in a gentle touch but then the embrace became firmer as I took his hand and pressed it to my breasts. He responded almost immediately and we were soon engaged in the most delicious kiss, our tongues flicking away in each other's mouths and our hands running all over each other's bodies.

In no time at all we had thrown off our clothes and I grasped his naked cock in my hand and gently pulled his foreskin back to reveal a fresh, pink knob, slightly glistening with moisture. Charlie possessed a really nice-looking prick, not too wide and not too big but, above all, it was really stiff, standing up from his thighs like a poker.

He may have been inexperienced, but he certainly knew how to pleasure a girl. He pulled me down onto the bed so I was lying on my back with my large, firm breasts and pouting little cunney lips, deliciously feathered with a golden bush, fully exposed to his view. He looked lovingly at me and then plunged his head downwards between my thighs. My juices were already flowing as he took each cunney lip in turn, sucking it gently, then probing my well-lubricated hole with his tongue, which made me writhe with delight.

'Oh, Oh, Oh!' I panted as he paid his devotions to the shrine of love by playfully taking little nips at my clitty, revelling in my creamy emissions. Oh, Charlie had the most divine tongue and I could have lain there for hours letting him eat my pussey. But I wanted to afford my new lover some relief, so I pulled his head away for a moment and lay beside him, kissing his face, his nipples and then working my way down to his rock-hard cock. With one sudden gulp I had his balls in my mouth and I massaged his cock to a straining new peak of erection whilst I licked and sucked his balls.

We moved round again so that my cunt was above his head and as I lowered myself down he wiggled his tongue around my crack as I transferred my own mouth to the tip of his huge cock. We lay sideways together in a perfect double gamahuche, or *soixante neuf* as the French have it, licking and sucking each other until my juices were flowing

6

so freely that I could not bear to be without a prick in my pussey. 'Oh, Charlie, Charlie, fuck me please, NOW!' I whispered fiercely.

Nothing loath, Charlie moved onto his knees as I lay down on my back, spreading my thighs as he took his cock in his hand and guided it towards my yearning cunt which was aching to be filled. His blunt, fleshy knob butted against the lips which opened to admit his tool, his whole eight inches sliding in to the hilt. I wrapped my legs round his waist and heaved up and down building up a marvellous rhythm to match Charlie's. Our bodies thrashed about with his mouth sucking on one engorged tittie and his hand squeezing the other. I raked his back with my nails as we came together, our juices mingling together as he pumped spouts of hot milky spunk into me and I climaxed beautifully, a shuddering spasm of pleasure running through every inch of my body.

Charlie rolled off me to lie panting with passion at my side. To my delight, I saw that his superb cock, all wet with my love juices was still full-looking, though not at its previous peak of hardness.

I rightly judged that if I kindled the spark, the fire would blaze again, so I let my hands wander over the cluster of thick blond hair around his tool and I let my mouth travel along that lovely blue vein that ran along the shaft to the uncovered dome at the end of his mushroom-shaped knob. His prick now looked more capable than before and, as you know, dear diary, you who are the sole repository of my most intimate thoughts, I just cannot resist fondling a fat cock. I love to feel it throb and swell as my hand grasps the shaft and begins rubbing it up and down. Very soon, Charlie's tool had swelled back to its former fine state of full erection and I gently kissed the purple dome as I eased his foreskin up and down until his strong young cock stood smartly straining upwards almost vertically to his tummy.

His cock began to throb in my mouth as I greedily gobbled the pulsating prick, moving my head backwards and

forwards as he moaned with pleasure. I began to give him
sharp little licks on his swollen shaft followed by a series of
quick kisses up and down the stem, encompassing his heavy
balls. I thrust his cock in and out of my mouth in a quicken-
ing rhythm, deep into my throat and out again with my
little pink tongue licking at the top of every stroke, lapping
up the drops of the creamy white fluid that were beginning
to ooze out of the tiny eye at the top of his knob.

Few men can prevent themselves spending too soon while
being sucked off and I could tell by the shuddering shaft
between my lips that Charlie was ready to squirt his spunk.
First came a few early shoots and then crash! My mouth
was filled with juicy, gushing foam as his cock bucked uncontrollably as I held it lightly between my teeth. I let the juice
flow sweetly down my throat, gently worrying his now
spongy knob with my tongue for maximum stimulation and
then gradually I allowed the slickly wet shaft to slide free.

But after a short rest, whilst we gathered our breath, I
was inclined to see whether my fine, new lover was capable
of a third joust. I took hold of his chunky cock and bending
forward began to nibble at the bulbous dome until it stood
stiffly up. I then left off my lubrication with a butterfly kiss
and turned over onto my belly, pushing out my firm young
bottom towards Charlie's glowing face.

I turned my head round to see my darling anoint the head
of his cock with spittle and then he gently inserted the
uncapped knob between my bum cheeks until he reached
my puckered little bum-hole. I relaxed myself to accom-
modate his knob which entered my tight rear-dimple and he
pushed in at least two or three inches of his cock as he
twiddled my nipples with his hands which were clasped
around me. He snaked his right hand downwards into my
silky bush and he massaged my clitty vigorously as he
worked his sturdy tool into my arse until I was corked to
the limit.

Now his lusty young cock plunged in and out, pumping
and sucking like the thrust of an engine. I reached back to

spread my cheeks even further as the pace quickened until Charlie shot jets of gushing jism that both warmed and lubricated my bottom-hole. As he spurted into me, he continued to work his prick back and forth so that it remained stiff until with a 'pop' he uncorked it from my twitching little arsehole.

I looked up at the clock and whispered to Charlie that the concert was due to start in just eight minutes – I had rightly surmised that the dear boy was duty bound to attend. We dressed in record time and Sub-Lieutenant Nicholas and I made our entrance just before the concert was about to start.

So, dear diary, I hardly need to relate how much I enjoyed the attentions of Charlie in my cabin after the concert, although the sweet lad had to leave me at half past eleven for the loneliness of his own quarters.

Well, it is now time to embrace the arms of Morpheus. There can be no doubt that there are many objects of interest to be seen every day on the ocean. Now it is a distant sail, anon it is a shoal of porpoises, occasionally even a shark or a whale whilst sea-birds – the graceful gull or the swift-flying stormy petrel – are with you every day of a summer voyage. Altogether, I know of nothing more charming or, withal, more healthful than a voyage in good weather across the Atlantic. But it takes a goodly thick prick like my Charlie's to make the trip truly a voyage to remember. What a shame that my lover will probably be unable to see me in New York, although I am certain I can rely on madcap Molly to ensure that my nights will be as lively as can be!

August 6th, 1884

Lessons in humility are among the earliest fruits of foreign travel. One soon learns that the world is a little bigger than it appeared at home, that the people who inhabit it have customs and ideas equal to ours, and that our tiny corner of the earth is a mighty small fragment indeed.

And I would add that there is no country in the world, except his own, through which a Britisher (as the Americans call us) will find it pleasanter to travel than the United States of America.

We are so kindly received, so hospitably entertained and, as I have found out, so affectionately treated that we feel as much at home as if we were back in Great Britain. Our cousins across the broad Atlantic scarcely regard us as strangers at all and certainly do not behave towards us in any reserved fashion. Every courtesy and attention is given to us and we are told to make ourselves, and are made to feel ourselves, perfectly at home.

If a visitor to the fair city of New York does not have a marvellous time, then surely it must be mainly his or her own fault?

Let me substantiate this opinion from my own experience. When we docked yesterday, my cousin Molly was unable to meet me as she had suffered a slight accident whilst descending from a carriage and her physician forbade her from putting a foot to the ground. So instead she sent one of her beaus, a most agreeable young man named Bertram Sand, to escort me to her house situated just off Fifth Avenue which adjoins the famous Central Park.

But I am writing of these events too hastily and we must return, dear diary, to the quayside where I espied this handsome young man holding up a large card with the words 'Miss Jennifer Everleigh' emblazoned upon it. I wondered why this total stranger was advertising my name in this fashion and I strode up to him.

He raised his hat as I approached him. 'Miss Everleigh?' he inquired in a most charming soft American voice which I later discovered was the accent of the New England area of this vast country. 'My name is Bertram Sand and I am a friend of your cousin Miss Molly Farquhar who unfortunately is indisposed and unable to meet you. But she has asked me to deputize for her and indeed ma'am, it is truly a very great pleasure for me to welcome you to the United States of America.'

After recounting details of Molly's accident, he passed over a letter from Molly to introduce Bertram to me. I recognized her handwriting immediately and I knew at once that his story was true.

'How kind of you, sir, to take the trouble of welcoming me to your shores,' I replied.

'I say again, Miss Everleigh, it is a pleasure to meet you. Molly told me that you were the prettiest girl in the family and she sure was not exaggerating!' he said in his friendly New World speech.

'Why, thank you, Mr Sand.' I said politely. 'Look, I have a porter here with my luggage piled upon a wheelbarrow. Have you a carriage waiting for us?'

'Certainly I have, ma'am,' he smiled as he waved to his coachman. 'Graham, you can load up now.' And he insisted on tipping the porter, although I had bought some American currency on the ship and was a little concerned to let a perfect stranger take on my own personal financial obligations, however trifling they may be. Yet somehow Bertram (which was very soon to be abbreviated to Bertie as was Jennifer to Jenny) was so friendly and natural that it seemed I had known him far longer than the two minutes since we had met and I did not feel badly about letting him slip some coins into the gnarled hand of the porter.

Graham was an excellent coachman and he kept a steady pace as I craned my neck out of the carriage to see for the first time the sights of New York. The new parts of New York are formed of straight lines and right angles. And the straight lines of the principal streets, coupled with the square and lofty buildings on each side of them, have a bewildering effect on the stranger. Broadway, for example, is a thoroughfare of immense length, of some six miles from end to end. Yet few but a native would be able to tell on striking it whether he was on the upper or the lower end, except from the numbers on the houses and shops.

We reached the centre of this fabulous city and I marvelled at the size and beauty of Central Park. From what I could see, it is laid out with great taste, planted with the choicest flowers and adorned with statues and busts of the world's worthies. And Fifth Avenue is probably the grandest street of its kind anywhere in the world if the noble character of the private houses erected on each side of it is anything to go by. Molly lived in a house on a street just off Fifth Avenue, which had been divided up into apartments for wealthy young ladies and which was run as a private club by the owners. Americans are great travellers and it was comforting for parents to know that they could journey to far-off cities leaving their daughters in such an establishment. Mind, if they had known of the goings-on behind the staid frontage of The Stuyvesant Club for Young Ladies they may not have taken such a sanguine view, even though membership was extremely difficult to obtain as candidates had to pass a rigorous examination as to their backgrounds. I am afraid there is almost as much snobbery amongst the wealthy in New York as there is back home in London. However, that is another affair and is not germane to this particular tale.

'Be nice to the housekeeper, Mrs Larson,' warned Bertie. 'She runs the place on extremely liberal lines but rightly asks for her wishes to be respected for otherwise there would be chaos. There are some twelve girls resident at any one time and you can imagine all the hullaballoo what with all the boys buzzing around the place at all hours.'

As I was staying with Molly, I was very pleased to hear that men were not forbidden to enter the portals of the Stuyvesant Club.

'Oh, far from it,' said Bertie, with a roguish twinkle in his eye. 'Actually, the rules of the club do forbid members of the male sex to enter its hallowed portals, but a five dollar bill passed discreetly to Mrs Larson will usually gain entrance as long as she can be assured of the reliability of the gentleman concerned.'

'That seems reasonable enough,' I said, and then I made the most dreadful slip of the tongue. I wanted to repeat the old Somerset saying that it only takes one pin to prick your finger but it must have been the excitement of the day that caused me to blurt out: 'Yes, it only takes one pin to finger your prick! I mean, one prick to um, er, ah, I think you know what I mean, Bertie.'

'Well, I hope I do,' said Bertie roaring with laughter and that set me off giggling so that great gales of merriment could be heard from our carriage as we reached our destination.

I blushed with embarrassment as Bertie escorted me into the Stuyvesant Club, but his infectious laughter caused me to giggle and then to laugh out almost as loudly – which certainly caused cousin Molly some puzzlement as she was sitting in an armchair in the hallway, ready to welcome me to the hallowed portals of the Club.

It was just as well that Molly was a sport because otherwise she might well have called for a doctor and a strait-jacket for, by now, Bertie and I were in hysterics. Then, to cap it all, the avuncular, portly figure of the head porter (whose name was Herbert, as I later found out), whilst coming over to us to inquire what was causing all the fun and games, slipped on the highly polished parquet floor and went arse over tip, bringing down a chair, a small table and Mrs Larson's secretary, a pretty young girl who was carrying a sheaf of papers which were sent all over the place!

This set us off again and this time we were joined by a group of other girls and Molly, who was still sitting in her chair, called out: 'Well, Jenny Everleigh, I do declare that you make a grand entrance! Welcome, dear cousin to New York!'

Bertie picked Herbert up and assisted Miss Angela to her feet. Fortunately, neither was seriously hurt, although Herbert sustained a nasty bump on his backside. Our merriment was quelled by the severe tones of a middle-aged lady dressed severely in a black dress who asked sharply as to what this commotion was all about. It was, of course, the dreaded Mrs Larson and I blanched when I thought of the awful first impression I must have made upon her. However, the silver-tongued Bertie gave her a beautific smile and said: 'It is all my fault, Mrs Larson. I was laughing rather too heartily and startled poor old Herbert who slipped whilst coming over to me to ask me, no doubt, to moderate the amount of noise I was making. He cannoned into poor Miss Angela who, as we speak, is busy collecting her papers to take into your office.

'Allow me to introduce you, ma'am, to Miss Jenny Everleigh from England. Miss Everleigh comes from one of the finest families in London. Her Aunt Portia, Lady Arkley, is a personal friend of the Prince of Wales, is that not correct Miss Everleigh?'

Sensing that a tone of snobbish, aristocratic superciliousness would impress Mrs Larson, I drew myself up to my full five feet seven inches and said in a languid voice: 'Yes, that is absolutely so, Mr Sand. Aunt Portia spends a great deal of time with His Royal Highness.'

The effect was somewhat spoiled by Molly murmuring: 'Yes, and she's probably even better acquainted with Sir Hal Finchley who fucks her every Thursday after dinner.'

It was as well that Mrs Larson did not overhear this *sotto voce* comment as she changed her demeanour and said: 'Oh, I see. Well, Miss Everleigh, welcome to the Stuyvesant Club. Your rooms will be ready by now as we were expecting you would arrive at about this time. I trust you had a pleasant journey?'

'Only if she had a good fuck,' muttered Molly, which made it even more difficult for me to keep a straight face. It transpired that Mrs Larson was slightly deaf which was why my cousin could take some liberties with her speech. So again, Molly's whisper was unheard as Mrs Larson smiled graciously and gave orders for my trunks to be placed in my rooms.

Molly and I exchanged great hugs and kisses and she said: 'Jenny, darling, I have an important appointment in about ten minutes. You know you wrote to me about how you were keeping an intimate diary, well, I have been doing the same thing and a gentleman I met at a dinner party last night happens to be a publisher and he expressed great interest in my writing. So he is calling round here soon to look at my work and see if he can publish it. Jenny, darling, I may soon be quite famous!'

It is just as well that this gentleman doesn't see my diary, I thought to myself!

'Let my help you unpack,' offered Bertie. 'Perhaps we can meet you later, Molly?'

'Yes, I shall be with Mr Fuster in the drawing room,' said Molly.

I had a shrewd suspicion that Bertie would like to divest some clothes other than those in my trunks, and I must admit that I did take a fancy to this good-looking boy. Once we were safely in my rooms and the door had closed behind Herbert the porter and his young assistant, Bertie put his arms round me and I turned my face up to his and we kissed. As soon as our lips met I knew that I would have to see what lay in store for me from the attractive bulge in his trousers. My legs were buckling beneath me and I was sure that my nipples were hardening and almost visibly jutting through the fine, cream cotton of my blouse.

Our first kiss was tender and gentle but then the next was urgent and we fell back together onto the bed, his hand

15

squeezing my breast and the hardness of his erection pressed into my thigh. We continued this passionate embrace as he carefully unbottoned my blouse and I could feel his excitement mount even further as he massaged my lovely firm breasts with their cherry titties. He moved his mouth from mine and lowering his head began to suck them, first one, then the other. Oh, what an exquisite feeling!

Then I felt his hand run up my thighs and now it was my turn to breathe harder as his long fingers slid into my drawers at the side and straight into my eager cunt. I could barely breathe with the excitement of it all and I was now on fire with unslaked desire. I parted my legs and lay back with his mouth still sucking an engorged tittie as his fingers glided in and out of my dampening cunney. I cooed with delight as he pulled down my drawers and began to rub my clitty. Then suddenly he stopped, looked up at me with a whimsical smile which I returned.

'Yes, please,' I murmured, and in no time at all we had torn off our clothes and were lying naked on the bed. I reached for his cock and I must confess that my heart thumped like mad when I reached out for it. What a magnificent prick! It was as smooth as silk yet as hard as ivory and what a length did my Bertie have the good fortune to possess – his superb shaft must have been fully nine inches long and I wondered if I could take all of this luscious pleasure stick inside me.

'Oh, Jenny, you are the most adorable girl,' Bertie whispered. 'As soon as I saw you, I fell in love with you and my cock has been at attention almost continually since you let me take your hand when you got into my carriage.'

'Well, now it is your turn to get into my carriage,' I smiled, lying back and opening my legs to prepare for his invasion. He put his giant prick against my moist love-channel and rubbed the knob against my cunney hair which I found immensely satisfying. But would I be able to take in his gigantic cock? He put his his cock against my cunney lips and with his hands on my hips he thrust forward gently, easing himself slowly inside my willing cunt.

I could hardly believe it but my juices were now flowing freely and this must have enabled Bertie to nudge in all nine inches of that great cock inside me. He pulled out and pushed in as I relaxed and began to enjoy myself. Now he went in and out in a steady rhythm, making my firm breasts bobble about with each thrust. Bertie worked his cock magnificently, slowly but surely getting it right up with every thrust giving me the benefit of the whole length with each stroke. I was in a new world in the New World as he slid in and out with such tremendously long, vigorous strokes, pumping away until I thought I would faint away with delight. But I did not swoon but very quickly spent in a veritable ecstacy of bliss as I screamed out my joy at the pleasure afforded me by such a delicious proof of American manliness.

He did not come at the same time but stopped and rested a minute or two. Then rising and keeping me still impaled upon his mighty cock, without losing place even for a single second, he turned me over and recommenced his divine moves, with his hands under me in front, frigging and tickling my clitty till I almost wrenched myself away from him by the violence of my convulsive contortions. To my surprise, Bertie then drew out his cock and with another plunge, he drove the head of his prick into my bum-hole, which was quite unexpected, though easy for him to reach in the position he had me.

'Ah! Oooh! Be careful, darling!' I cried out, as I was worried that his huge prick might rend me. But his busy fingers were adding to my erotic madness by the artistic way in which they groped within my sopping cunt and almost immediately Bertie sent gushings of boiling spunk into my bum, inundating the sensitive sheath which enclosed him so tightly.

What a grand love-making session we enjoyed though I did tell dear Bertie that next time he should spunk into my cunt. 'I thought you would prefer a bottom-fuck, my darling Jenny,' said my gallant young Yankee. 'I did not know whether the time of the month was propitious for fucking and I did not want you to worry about such matters whilst you were on vacation. But if you like, let's fuck again in five minutes and this time I promise I'll spend in your cunt!'

And he fulfilled that promise, dear diary, with great style! Indeed, I complimented Bertie on his ability to fuck like a rattlesnake, as the Yankees say, though whether those horrible reptiles actually possess any peculiar prowess in this field is a matter, alas, with which I am not familiar.

However, young Bertram Sand was more than pleased to accept my compliment. 'It is most kind of you to praise my love-making,' he said, 'Mind, I must in all fairness tell you that my cousin Graham is even better between the sheets than me. He has the advantage of a quite enormous prick and enjoys a great amount of stamina, which is surprising as he is of a sedentary disposition being a great reader. His uncle, Colonel Pugh, has a huge ranch down in Texas and allows Graham twenty-five dollars a week just to spend on buying books for the ranch-house library. Of course, this means that he spends a lot of time browsing along the Broadway bookshops some of which, Jenny, are unsuitable for young ladies.'

'You should see the print-shops in Hollywell Street in London,' I retorted. 'Or go to Hotten's bookshop in Piccadilly which my friend Sir Andrew Scott tells me has the finest collection of erotica in Europe. Don't worry about offending my sensibilities, dear Bertie, I am not one of your damsels that swoons at the sight of a bare arm – or even a bare arse!'

We laughed gaily as we dressed and went downstairs to meet Molly and Mr Fuster, the publisher who had expressed such deep interest in her diaries. But though we searched through all the public rooms, we could not see her anywhere.

'I'll ask old Herbert if Molly went out with this guy,' said Bertie. I waited in the hall whilst he found the porter but I failed to see my madcap cousin anywhere. Bertie returned in a few moments looking rather puzzled. 'I just don't know where she can be,' he said. 'Herbert says he saw a young man talking to her in the main lounge but they haven't left the club.'

'I know where they can be found,' I chuckled. 'At least, I have a pretty fair idea, especially if Mr Fuster is a red-blooded young publisher!'

'You don't mean to say they have gone upstairs to Molly's room?' he gasped.

'And pray, why not? You took me upstairs after a very brief acquaintance,' I said.

'My, you English girls are something else,' murmured Bertie admiringly.

'Well, there's little point beating about the bush, is there, my darling? If a girl wants to be fucked, why should she be coy about it? On the other hand, though, a gentleman must accept that "no" means "no" and however randy he may feel, the wishes of his enamourata must be respected. If she has led him to believe that he may reach his goal, I do think that any girl worth her salt will make her boyfriend happy by giving him a good tossing-off. However, it is purely a matter of discretion, Bertie, and I am afraid that far too many young men try to pressurize us into fucking. In the last resort, men are stronger but there is no pleasure in taking a female aganist her will,' I continued.

'I so agree with you,' said Bertie warmly. 'There is a thrill in the chase for both hunter and hunted but the climax must be a matter of mutual desire.'

'Yes, there is no doubt at all that men who treat their partners with consideration will enjoy fucking much more than the brutes who simply threaten or cajole,' I added as we reached the door of Molly's room which was festooned with a 'Do Not Disturb' notice hanging over the doorknob.

'Ah ha,' smiled Bertie. 'You were right, Jenny. They are obviously inside enjoying an interesting, ah, editorial meeting!'

'No, I don't think so,' I said. 'I think they are simply having a good fuck.'

Bertie laughed out loud and said: 'You know, Jenny, Molly told me that there was something the matter with the lock on this door. Old Herbert took it out this morning and won't replace it until tonight, so they really are taking quite a chance in there.'

'You aren't suggesting . . .?'

'I do like to see a good-looking young couple fucking,' admitted Bertie. 'Yet I am not a voyeur, as I far prefer to participate. Indeed, the reason I would like to go in, if I may be absolutely frank, is that we might be invited to join in. You may not believe this, but I have never fucked Molly and would dearly love the opportunity to do so.

'We did find ourselves locked together in an embrace last Thursday but her monthly period had not yet finished and she prefers not to take cock during that time.'

'So you acted like the perfect gentleman and did not attempt to force her to fuck against her will?' I interposed.

'Of course I didn't press the issue,' said Bertie. 'In fact, dear Molly did offer to suck my cock but I declined the kind gesture as it would have been like eating the most delicious *hors d'oevres* without partaking of the main course.'

'In that case,' I said firmly, 'I think you deserve that *plat du jour*,' and I slowly and quietly opened the door.

Dear diary, I was not surprised to see what was going on in Molly's room – though perhaps Molly and the handsome Mr Fuster were more startled that someone had disregarded the unequivocal notice to keep out, especially as both were stark naked!

Anyway, this slim young man had placed Molly on her back with her bottom projecting over the edge of the bed, her thighs stretched wide open and her legs resting on his shoulders. I could see his tight little bum working vigorously back and forward, driving his prick in and out between the moist lips of Molly's cunt.

'Oh, yes, that's lovely!' Molly cried out. 'Push it in well. Yes, yes, yes, Oh!'

'Oh, good golly, Miss Molly,' gasped Mr Fuster. 'Oh,

what a delicious cunt you have, my sweet. Such inviting thick lips and such a lovely warm, wet cunney that holds my prick like a glove!'

'Ah, Harry! Harry! Fuck me harder! You must not be frightened! Fuck me as hard as you are able! Push your fat cock up my cunt!' screamed out Molly. Her buttocks rose up to meet his thrusts until both appeared to come together in a luscious spend.

Harry lay across the lovely girl, panting with exhaustion but he gave an embarassed self-conscious little yelp when he saw that they had received two unexpected visitors. Darling Molly was quite unconcerned, of course, and all she said was: 'Put a chair against the door, Bertie. I don't mind you two watching us but I don't want to fuck in front of the servants.'

Bertie did as she requested and we made our introductions. It turned out that Bertie was a great friend of Simon Fuster, Harry's older brother and we chatted away happily as we helped ourselves to the champagne Molly had smuggled up to her room. She rightly insisted that we divested ourselves of our clothes if we were planning on staying. I had no objection, for not only did I know full well that Bertie wanted to fuck Molly, I was quite taken by the dark, good looks of Harry Fuster, a youth of only nineteen and I rather relished the idea of sucking his fine young cock up to full erection. Luckily, neither Molly nor I are at all jealous of each other's beaus and, in any case, we enjoy keeping things in the family!

Molly must have been reading my mind as she suddenly said: 'Jenny, Harry has fucked me very nicely indeed. I'm sure with just a little encouragement, he would do the same for you, won't you, darling?'

'I would be only too happy to oblige,' said Harry gallantly. So I took his hand and pressed it to my breasts. For a moment, he looked startled but then he responded and in a trice were engaged in a most passionate kiss which fairly sucked the breath out of my heaving lungs. He ran his hands across my hardening nipples and then slid them down my belly to my swollen pussey lips as he lowered his head to take those sweet titties in his watering mouth, his tongue flickering wildly over my erect little nipples.

I grasped hold of his naked cock which was now sticking up stiffly to attention. I gave it a friendly little rub and then ever so gently ran my fingernails up and down the shaft. I love to fondle a good stiff prick and I felt the shaft throb and swell as I continued my ministrations. Harry continued to nuzzle my titties as he began to finger my now soaking pussey, tickling my clitty and rousing all my passions to fever point. He kept his fingers busy frigging my cunt as I rose up to lean over him, positioning my supple young bum almost over his face and I opened my legs so that he could enjoy a good view of my cunney.

I began to kiss his belly and quickly worked my way down to his cock which I continued to stroke as I took his mushroomed red knob in my mouth and sucked firmly on it. This is the most sensitive part of a boy's prick and I did not want poor Harry to spend outside my pussey so after a few salacious sucks, I transferred my lips to his hairy balls each of which I gave a good licking as the clever boy grasped my bum cheeks, forcing them downwards so that he could lick my cunt in a superbly executed double gamahouche.

He licked and lapped all along my cunney lips and inside my crack until he found my clitty and he rolled his tongue around it allowing me to enjoy the most exquisite sensation throughout my body.

Then at exactly the same time, as if our minds were as one for no words were exchanged, we moved round to enjoy a mouth to mouth kiss and I felt the urgent swell of his thick cock against my mossy mound. My fingers travelled down his back whilst I opened my legs to feel his balls against my thighs. He raised himself slightly on to his hands and then thrust that flagpole of a prick firmly into my juicy cunt. The lunge and thrust was quite perfect and my cunney burst open like a water lily as his shaft slid up my love-channel. Our hairy triangles mingled as he pumped his prick in and out of my willing pussey. In and out rammed his cock with great squelchy sounds as our juices slurped together and we quickened our rhythm as I sensed by his shuddering that he was approaching the very highest point of excitement. I bucked my hips to meet every thrust, to achieve the maximum contact with that marvellous tool. I threw my head back in abandon as my own climax coursed through my body and seconds later Harry reached his own peak of pleasure as he pumped spurt after spurt of hot jism inside me, sending further waves of ecstacy through every fibre of my being.

He then pulled out his cock which was glistening with its coating of love-juices. I swooped down and sucked the very last morsels of spendings from the tip of his cock which slipped slowly back into its normal flaccid state and the red-capped dome slithered back inside its covering of foreskin.

This beautifully performed act of *l'arte de faire l'amour* had obviously aroused Bertie, whose big cock was sticking up so grandly against his belly whilst Molly's blood was also afire as she caressed her own pussey lips saying: 'Now it's my turn.'

I lay back to rest and closed my eyes but I felt soft lips resting gently at first and then with increasing urgency on my own. I opened my mouth beneath the persuasive pressure and a pert little tongue found its way between my teeth. This was strange, I thought, as neither Bertie nor Harry kissed in such fashion. I blinked and to my great surprise found that it was none other than Molly who was kissing me with such delightful charm. As you know, diary, I still and always will maintain that a nice stiff cock cannot be beaten but variety is the spice of life so I raised no objection when I felt a warm friction journeying knowingly from the base of my throat to the valley between my firm, jutting breasts. Molly moved her head quite expertly as I whimpered as her probing mouth and fingers played on my body with a sure and sensitive touch. Our limbs entwined as our bodies plunged into delight that ebbed and flowed.

Molly softly rubbed my titties as my nipples stiffened. My own hands were on her shoulders, caressing and stroking as her hands pulled my long white legs apart, nuzzling her full lips around my blonde thatch of damp pubic hair. She giggled and slipped out from between my legs and turned round into that *soixante neuf* position I had just enjoyed with Harry. So now her pussey was directly over my face as she pushed her pert bum outwards as she bent downwards to kiss my wet cunney lips. My pussey seemed to open wide as she slipped her tongue through the pink lips, licking between the inner grooves of my slit in long, thrusting strokes.

I clasped Molly's lovely buttocks and pulled them apart to reach the soft lips of her cunt which like mine was covered with light, golden hair. Then I began to lap at her cunney lips and I trembled with pleasure as my tongue sought out and found the secrets of her cherry-coloured quim. Her juices dribbled like honey from her parted labia and her clitty turned from pale pink to deep red as I flicked gently with the wet tip of my darting little tongue. I excited the sweet girl so much that she stopped playing with my cunt and raised her head, panting with joy. 'Ohhh!' she screamed out. 'That's it! that's it!' as I worked my tongue until my jaw ached. I continued to tongue her juicy cunney, working my tongue deeper and deeper into her hole. Her pussey was creaming with pleasure, the hot juice running all over my mouth and I felt I was half-drowning in an ocean of excitement until, heaving violently, the lovely girl got off a tremendous orgasm as her bum cheeks jerked feverishly in my hands until her frenzy subsided and I gently eased her soft body down to my side.

Now it was my turn to lay back on the bed with my legs apart and Molly rolled over on top of me and our breasts crushed together and our sopping mounds rubbed furiously against each other. Molly slipped a finger into my soaking pussey and rubbed harder and harder until my little clitoris turned as hard as a miniature prick to her touch. She slid a second then a third finger, spreading the lips apart as I moaned with sheer delight. Her head was drawn irresistably down and soon she was lapping away with all her might.

Molly's clever tongue probed and loved, darted and caressed my pussey. She too was pleased at the response she was getting from me as her tongue moved faster and faster, her hands kneading and spreading me wider and wider as I gasped with joy. My cunt was now gushing love-juice and each time she tongued me, my clitty stiffened, ever more eager and pulsating, wanting more and more as I squeezed her head between my thighs, urging her on as I felt myself on the brink of the ultimate pleasure as waves of lust ran up and down my spine.

'Aaaah! Aaaah! You've made me come!' I panted as I spent profusely all over Molly's mouth and chin, soaking her face with my juices which she greedily slurped and swallowed as I continued one of the most delicious and longest spend I have ever experienced. I must admit, dear diary, that though I still prefer cock above all, on the whole, if you will pardon the pun, girls somehow know how to lick out pussies far more stylishly than male lovers.

All this girlish sexual play had aroused both our boys and neither could prevent their hands straying to their cocks which they were pumping up and down with total uninhibition. 'Don't waste it!' cried Molly and she tore away Harry's hand and knelt down to take the firm, stiff shaft in her mouth. She gave a quick little moistening tonguing to the purple dome and then sucked at least three inches of his thick shaft into her mouth. I knew Molly was an excellent cocksucker and Harry was in a seventh heaven of delight as her mouth worked up and down, licking the entire length of his shaft, her hand grasping the base as she pumped her head up and down, keeping her lips taut, kissing and sucking and licking until Harry's prick began to twitch uncontrollably and with a cry he shot huge globs of white warm spunk into her mouth. Molly jammed her mouth over the twitching mushroomed knob and gulped and sucked every drop of jism from Harry's gushing prick until at last she fell away, gasping and licking her lips.

'Oh, your sperm tastes so invigorating, my darling. I cannot wait for this evening when we shall again be together and you may fuck me all through the night!'

I smiled my approval and would have given Bertie's lovely cock a good sucking but the dear lad could contain himself no longer and his hand moved faster and faster up and down his shaft though just before he climaxed I managed to clamp my lips over his knob and swallowed hard in anticipation. How correct my judgement was, for after a few early shoots of salty spunk, crash! My mouth was filled with lovely gushing foam as his cock bucked from side to side while I lightly held it between my teeth. I had to suck and swallow at great pace to drain the liquor from Bertie's magnificent cock. Then I felt the textured tool soften as I rolled my lips around the head of the shaft and I nibbled at the funny round bulb until my young man lay drained.

'Does his spunk taste nice?' inquired Molly, smacking her lips. 'I do so enjoy swallowing sperm. Nothing tastes as clean and as fine as those boiling spurts of cream.'

I nodded in agreement and said: 'Yes, I too adore a man who can squirt jets of juice into my mouth. I am so often surprised to find that some girls find it distasteful.'

'It is a perfectly natural and enjoyable act as far as I am concerned,' commented Molly. 'However, my dear, it would never do if we all liked exactly the same thing. No doubt there are love-making acts that others enjoy that I would find boring or even worse. As you know, Lady Margaret Fennise likes to be soundly whipped before fucking. I cannot think of anything more silly – or more painful!'

'There is no accounting for taste,' Bertie chipped in. 'Why, do you know that here in New York there is a high-class madam, Mrs Oxford, who specializes in giving out whippings to her clients?'

'I have heard about Mrs Oxford's establishment,' said Harry. 'I hear that sometimes it is the men who want to whip the girls, but more often they actually pay good money for the girls to whip them!'

'They have peculiar ideas to my way of thinking. All I can suppose that in their minds they like to hark back to when they were children and nanny put them over her knee to have their bottoms smacked, something from which they derived a perverse pleasure,' he added.

'Don't be too hard on them,' urged Molly. 'I don't mind having my bottom smacked, so long as it's not too hard. Unfortunately, I had a lover, Lieutenant Dalgliesh of the 69th Sussex Lancers, Jenny, who let matters get out of hand, so to speak! After bringing up the cheeks of my bum to a fine reddish hue, he then proceeded to prise open my buttocks and tried to coax the plump head of his cock into my arsehole. I don't mind this occasionally, but not even my cunt was ready and we just did not extract the fullest pleasure from our jousting.'

'Jenny and I were talking about this subject just before we came in here,' said Bertie. 'We agreed that whilst it can be great fun, making sexual intercourse even more exciting, nothing should be done without one's partner's total consent. I suppose that I must be rather dull. Straightforward fucking is the game for me, together with the nice, straight things you can do together that give pleasure to both me and my girl.'

'I like that attitude,' said Molly seriously. 'In fact, I think that British men could learn a great deal from their American cousins.

'I have found that deference to our sex is nigh universal here. I doubt whether there is another city in the world, not even in Paris, where so much attention is paid to the ladies as it is shown in New York. They are always politely attended, rarely incommoded in any way in their comings and goings, with separate entrances being provided for them in hotels, railway stations and other public places. The fact that brutal assaults on women are rare in New York goes to show that respect for us is founded in the genuine sentiment of the people.

'Indeed, I would even say that the age of chivalry, now gone from Europe, has taken fresh root in America which is quite, quite splendid. So splendid, indeed, that I shall suck on your prick, Harry Fuster, until it swells up as stiff as a poker and as hard as a rock. Then I shall graciously permit you to fuck me.'

Alas, dear Bertie had a prior engagement with his cousin Graham, he of the enormous cock, if Bertie's comment was true, and indeed I took the opportunity of hoping that the two young men were not joining up for anything but business. Bertie smiled and said that he had simply promised his cousin to meet him on some trifling matter of business and before we took leave of Molly and Harry, we arranged to dine that night at one of the smart Fifth Avenue hotels.

We dressed and quietly left Molly and Harry to continue their fucking in private. Oh, what a grand introduction to love-making in the New World I had enjoyed. The tenderness of those hours will ever remain with me. What did Virgil write, diary? Ah, yes. *Ne tamen urit amor; quis enim adsit amori.**

*Love consumes me yet – for what bound can be set to love?

August 7th, 1884

It is commonly understood that the high rate of wages
prevailing in the United States of America has led to a
greater adaptation of mechanical appliances to all the purposes for which machinery can be used than would otherwise have been the case.

Without doubt, American inventors are wonderfully ingenious and their notions find a ready market all over the
world. It is to America that we are largely indebted for
many of the labour-saving machines now in common use.
Nothing that can be possibly done by machinery is done by
hand in this marvellous country.

The Americans are no slouches when it comes to pressing
these inventions into active service. Indeed, our cousins are
very much in advance of ourselves when it comes to adapt-
ing to the various concerns of life the mechanical discoveries
of our time.

For example, even comparatively insignificant towns in
America avail themselves of the most recent invention of
the age, the telephone. There are towns here that are little
more than villages that contain fifty to sixty citizens, yet
who participate in the advantages of telephonic com-
munication.

According to statistics recently published by the International Telephone Company, more than double the
number of persons subscribe for the use of the apparatus in
New York than in London, though the former city has
scarcely a quarter the population of the latter.

This morning I had cause to be thankful for this fact. I
was brushing my teeth when I felt a sharp twinge of discomfort. A back tooth in the top set had given me some

trouble a month or two back and my London dentist, Mr Peter Ferdenzi, had indeed warned me that in all probability the tooth would have to be extracted. I ate breakfast with care, biting only gingerly into the delicious hot buttered toast. I was sitting alone because Molly was suffering from a headache (I could only offer superficial sympathy because the night before she had consumed two bottles of champagne and three brandies before collapsing into Harry's arms). Dear Bertie was going to take me on a trip round Manhattan so I did not mind being by myself.

Spot on ten o'clock Bertie appeared but as I rose to greet him, my tooth really began to ache quite horribly. I grimaced and Bertie said: 'Jenny, are you quite well?'

'I have a wretched toothache, my darling,' I confessed.

'A toothache? Well, there is no point sitting around just hoping it will disappear of its own accord. You must come with me to the dentist.'

Now I have a fear, quite irrational, of dentists. I have always been to see Mr Ferdenzi in Harley Street once a year whether or not I needed treatment, for prevention is better than a cure. I have never been actually hurt by Mr Ferdenzi or any other dentist but I have a dread of the drill and other instruments of torture, and I confessed this to Bertie.

'I quite understand, my sweet Jenny,' he cried. 'But the sooner we make an appointment for you, the quicker we shall be able to stop the pain. I know just the man for you to see. He is the best dentist in New York, as well as being a personal friend of mine. His name is Ronald Donne and I guarantee that he will not injure your poor mouth in any serious fashion.'

'Is he a good dentist?' I enquired.

'As I said, Jenny, he is the best in New York. All the top people in town go to him.'

'Then I will send a message to see when I can make an appointment.'

'No need to delay, darling. He is on the telephone. I will call him straightaway and ensure that he will fit you in.'

I nodded my agreement though in truth I was not totally enamoured with the thought of seeing Mr Donne so quickly. Then I thought to myself, come now, Jenny, don't be a coward. Remember you are British! Don't let the Yankees see that you are scared!

In just a few moments, Bertie was back with a big grin on his face. 'Marvellous news, Jenny. Ronnie has had a cancellation and will be free in half an hour. My carriage is at the door so just put on your hat and I'll take you there. You will like Ronnie, he really is a very charming gentleman.'

By now my tooth was really giving me quite a lot of pain so I did not even attempt any delaying tactic but put on my hat and coat and strode out into the warm sunshine. Although it was high summer, the temperature was fortunately not oppressively high. I gazed out across the street to look at the fine buildings but the journey was unpleasant because Broadway was full of holes and ruts that must have been trying to the horses, and was certainly extremely trying to the passengers.

However, we arrived at Mr Donne's surgery and to my surprise Bertie did not follow me in but said: 'Jenny, I am afraid that I have an urgent business appointment. I would not have been able to take you out this morning, so while I am dreadfully sorry about your tooth, if it had to happen, it was better that it should happen today. I will pick you up later and take you and Ronnie out to luncheon.'

I was a little put out by this somewhat cavalier attitude and was feeling more than a little irritated when Mr Donne came into the hallway to greet me.

My heart missed a beat when I saw the dentist – it was a very different feeling than I experienced when I visited Mr Ferdenzi, a middle-aged gentleman well into his fifties. Mr Donne must have been in his mid-forties, not too tall, but with a powerful stocky figure, a handsome, rugged face and he was blessed with twinkling blue eyes from which radiated a very, very sensual attraction.

'Miss Jenny Everleigh? I am Ronald Donne. A pleasure to

31

meet such a beautiful friend of Bertie, even though I know that you would have preferred a meeting away from this place!' he said with a grin.

'I suppose Bertie has told you that I am something of a coward,' I smiled back, as we walked through into the surgery.

'Oh, don't worry, Miss Everleigh, I promise that you will not feel any more than a passing discomfort,' said the handsome dentist as I sat somewhat gingerly in his chair. 'I give you my word that I could not harm such a pretty English rose.'

'I am glad to hear that for I am a rose that does not wish to be plucked,' I said somewhat mischievously.

'I beg your pardon,' said Mr Donne who had turned away to slip on a white coat.

'I have no wish to be plucked!' I repeated.

'I will not pluck you,' he promised.

No, but you could do something quite similar, I thought as I lay back in the chair opening my mouth to let this good-looking man take a close look inside it.

Within a very few moments Mr Donne made up his mind and I knew immediately from his kindly but somewhat sorrowful expression what to expect.

'I am sorry Miss Everleigh, but that tooth will have to come out. There is nothing else for it. The alternative is to suffer more and more pain, and in the end it will still have to be extracted. Fortunately, you will not notice its loss and nor will it be noticed by any of your many admirers.'

'Oh, no!' I cried, 'I have never had a tooth out before.'

'Not to worry,' said Mr Donne cheerfully. 'I will simply give you a whiff of gas and bingo! All will be done and you will not feel a thing. The tooth is somewhat loose so I really can say that afterwards there will only be some minor discomfort for which I will prescribe a powder. Now, tell me, did you have a big breakfast this morning?'

'No, just some toast and coffee.'

'Good. I shall administer some nitrous oxide. But first I

had better examine your chest to ensure that your heart and lungs are sound.'

I sat up, took off my jacket and unbuttoned my blouse. I was wearing nothing underneath because the weather was fine, so my uptilted young breasts were almost bared. As he put the rubber end of his stethoscope on my left breast, I could feel my nipples hardening up to point proudly out under their thin, white linen covering.

'Fine, fine,' he muttered. 'As I expected, all is well. You had, er, better button your blouse as the sight of your lovely, um, er, figure might distract me.'

'Oh, I don't mind distracting you,' I said truthfully. 'If you take out this tooth without hurting me, I shall do my best to distract you as best I can – and that's a promise!'

'Really, well let's not waste any time,' he said and placed the gas mask over my face.

Well, diary, as we know, dear Ronnie (as I later called him) was as good if not better than his word. I experienced a strange sensation as the gas began its journey through my body. There was a loud rushing noise in my head and I dreamed a funny, old scene. I cannot quite recall it exactly, but I thought I was riding one of those roundabout horses one sees at a fairground. I felt that I was unconscious for only a few seconds, though in truth the tooth was more obstinate than Ronnie had believed and I was under the influence for some five minutes.

I came to feeling a little groggy at first, but otherwise quite well. Ronnie was standing over me with a glass of water in his hand.

'Woosh this round your mouth,' he ordered, 'and then spit it out into the basin. We'll do this a few times until the bleeding stops.'

In no time at all, I was my old self. I was so happy and grateful to Ronnie that I told him that I wanted to show my gratitude. From the bulge underneath the white coat, I could see that something in the *l'arte de faire l'amour* stakes would more than compensate my lovely new man.

'Would you like to change your role?' I asked boldly.

'Why, what do you mean, Miss Everleigh?'

'It's Jenny, and you are Ronnie are you not? Well, instead of working at an extraction, how about making an insertion for a change?'

I stood up, unbuttoned my blouse and shrugged it off, exposing my naked breasts to his delighted gaze. I kicked off my shoes and sat down again to peel off my stockings. I unhooked my skirt and let it drop to the floor and slowly, somewhat tantalisingly pulled down my knickers to give Ronnie a full-frontal view of my mossy blonde bush.

He gaped as I struck a coquettish pose and said: 'Well, do you like what you see, or do you wish to send the goods back to the manufacturer?'

The speed with which he tore off his clothes soon showed me this was an unnecessary question to have asked! We embraced passionately and we locked our tongues together in each other's mouths as we kissed with such vigour that I felt in danger of sliding to the floor. I took hold of Ronnie's prick and took a few paces back where I had noticed there was a large sofa. I sat down, still holding his prick and gave it a gentle rub. My, it was thick! Dear Ronnie had one of the thickest cocks I had ever seen, despite the fact that he was circumcised (I later found out that he was of the Jewish persuasion) and it throbbed violently in my hand. I was both shocked and excited, and I had to tell him that I had never held such a big prick.

He smiled and pulled my head gently towards this stiff monster. I wet my lips with my tongue as I decided to give Ronnie the most delicious sucking off he would ever experience.

I began by licking all round his pulsing, mushroom knob and then I moved down the sides as I stroked his big balls. Then I sucked the knob gently into my mouth and, with a quick change of pace, began to lash my tongue round this gorgeous cock-shaft. I sucked in so much that his knob was almost touching the back of my throat, as I struggled to

34

enclose more of that huge shaft. I massaged the underside with my tongue and gave his balls a gentle squeeze as his hands caressed their way through my thick mane of hair.

Almost immediately Ronnie jerked and went rigid and his thick prick spunked jets of hot, sticky fluid that I greedily swallowed until I had milked every delicious drop of love juice from his still stiff prick.

Then I laid myself face downwards on the sofa, and jerked my lithe little bum in the air, opening my legs to give Ronnie a good view of my moistening cunt. I rubbed myself lasciviously between my legs and felt the juices welling up inside me. I turned my head and saw Ronnie on his knees behind me, already positioning his cock between my arse-cheeks, ready to drive it home between them.

And oh, his thick shaft plugged and stretched my pussey in an incredible fashion, his cock moving in slow rhythmic thrusts and my body fairly thrilling with rapture as he buried his cock deep inside my dripping cunney. I felt his large, pendulous balls bang against the back of my thighs as he thrust forward urgently and then I felt the first waves of orgasm coursing their way through my body as with a crash, dear Ronnie spunked off copiously, filling my cunney with its first taste of warm sperm that day.

But amazingly, Ronnie's giant cock refused to go limp! It still remained semi-erect so I sucked the monster tool back to its magnificent firmness and made him roll onto his back. Then I straddled him, pumping my pussey up and down his shaft whilst he cupped my full, firm breasts, flicking the rosy little nipples between his fingers. This time it took a little longer before we both spent together, his squirts of spunk mingling happily with a final gush of my own pussey juices.

We were now both exhausted and Ronnie grinned as I tugged at his limp, wet cock.

'The spirit is willing but the flesh is weak,' he commented.

'I am not dissatisfied with your performance,' I said. 'I

just wondered whether it would be possible to fuck again before luncheon.'

'Certainly, my sweet little poppet! But I do need some time to recuperate and in any case I have a patient to see in about five minutes. Look, gather up your things and let me take you through to the recovery room. Sometimes, my patients need a rest after treatment especially when I have been forced to extract a tooth. There is a nice bed there on which I will join you as soon as I have finished with my next patient, Marie Hartland. Actually, you may know Miss Hartland, she is a friend of your cousin Molly and I believe is also acquainted with Bertie Sand.'

'I don't think I have had the pleasure.'

'Oh, never mind. She is a most delicious young lady with the most voluptuous intimate tastes. Well, so I have been told,' he added hastily.

I smiled as Ronnie helped me pick up my clothes and we kissed as I lay down on the very comfortable bed in the recovery room. Indeed, it was so comfortable and I had so exhausted myself by that lovely fucking match with the randy dentist, that within minutes I was dozing peacefully away.

I enjoyed this brief rest which was disturbed by the soft click of the doorlatch. 'Come here, Ronnie,' I murmured sleepily. 'Go down on me, darling and eat my pussey.'

There was no reply but I heard the rustle of someone undressing and of clothes dropping to the floor. And as I lay on my back I felt my knees being gently parted and a pillow being slipped under my buttocks.

'M'mmm, that's nice,' I purred, as a soft hand stroked my silky blonde bush.

'Oh, oh, oh, that is very nice indeed,' I added, as the hand continued its journey and a long finger began to press through my moistening cunney lips.

I was really enjoying this stimulation which began in earnest when I felt a head push between my legs and a warm, wet tongue began to lick at my cunt. My excitement grew as I felt the lips pressing down on my juicy love-nest and I grasped what I thought would be Ronnie's head to encourage him further. But to my amazement, I reached out to grasp a full head of feminine curls and for the first time since this episode began I opened my eyes.

What a surprise! For instead of Ronnie, I found myself being gamahuched by a strange girl! This was obviously the Marie Hartland who possessed 'the most voluptuous intimate tastes'. She was a pretty if somewhat buxom girl, whose head was topped with a mass of dark auburn hair. So intent was she on kissing my cunney that she did not even desist to effect a formal introduction.

But how well could Marie suck pussey! This is a sadly neglected art, especially in England, where boys are not encouraged to perform this delicate love-play as they are on the Continent or indeed in the East. I have always enjoyed being sucked off so I lay back and enjoyed the delicious sensations.

I almost screamed with pleasure as Marie's clever tongue found the mark and I pushed my silky-haired mound up against her face as she began licking harder at my clitty as her fingers prised open my pussy lips. She sank first one then two fingers slowly into my juicy hole, making me gasp and tremble as she eased them deeper and deeper inside me.

Her tongue and fingers were thrilling me and my cunt was tingling with a really intense excitement that pulsated through my whole body. She twisted her fingers round as she thrust them inside me, and I felt the first stirrings of an orgasm as she licked harder at my little clitty, raising it up to a jutting hard peak as her fingers pushed in further and faster in and out of my cunney. As I felt myself coming, I writhed wildly against her, holding her head firmly against my pussey with one hand while I squeezed at my nipples with the other.

The fabulous pressure of Marie's tongue and fingers kept me at the peak of excitement for what seemed to be a deliciously long time, and even when my climax eventually subsided, I still felt very aroused and eager to continue.

So when Marie whispered: 'Would you be a dear and finish me off, please?', I was more than happy to oblige. I laid the girl down on her back and admired her large breasts over which I cupped my hands, rubbing up her rosy titties to little peaks of hardness under my palms. Then I twisted myself round to sit across her with my bum directly over her face and I bent forward to begin returning some of the pleasure she had given me.

I parted her cunney lips through the mossy bush of curly black hair and carefully examined her pussey lips.

I gave the furry bush a thorough tongueing, soaking her pubic hair with my sweet saliva and then slowly I worked my tongue deeper and deeper into her cunney. At the same time I could feel her tongue licking its way round my own quim, tickling its way round my cunney lips and flicking delightfully in and out of my cunt. I buried my head in her mound, lapping and sucking her sopping cunt with my bottom jerking feverishly up and down in response to the beautiful tickling of Marie's tongue.

My pussey was creaming with pleasure, the hot juice running between my thighs and I was half-drowning in an ocean of excitement in this fiery sexual encounter, when a strange new sensation assailed my senses. Unless I was much mistaken, I heard the bedsprings twang and a third body was now joining in our fun! It must be Ronnie, I thought to myself, but I was far, far too busy muff-diving on Marie's lovely cunt to care too much.

The new arrival was crouching across Marie and his arms were then wrapped round my breasts, tweaking away at my titties. Then I felt the sturdy head of his cock sliding in between my bum-cheeks to force its way to the edge of my arsehole. Could I take this cock up my arse whilst being sucked off at the same time?

I drew breath and then resumed my attentions to Marie's cunt, placing one hand under her bum for elevation and the other reaching around her thigh so I could spread her cunt-lips with my thumb and middle finger. I place my lips over her swollen clitty and sucked it into my mouth where the tip of my tongue began to explore it from all directions. I could feel it growing larger and her legs wiggling and twitching up and down while I ministrated my affections upon her.

Meanwhile, Marie began to tongue round my own dripping pussey, pausing just for a moment to suck upon the pair of pendulous balls belonging to our new friend as he wet his shaft with some pomade which would aid his attack upon my rear. He slowly eased his cock inside me. At first there was some discomfort, but then he was fucking my bum-hole with vigour as with one hand he flicked away at my titties and with the other frigged at my clitty, which was engorged with this three-way excitement.

All too soon we reached the peaks and we screamed loudly in the frenzy of emission and I actually fainted away with delight as I felt a gush of spunk spurt into my bum. I soon recovered, but to my astonishment I discovered that the owner of the cock that had just popped out of my bottom was not, as I had thought, randy Ronnie, but another handsome young gentleman who I had never met before in my life!

'Good heavens!' I exclaimed. 'Who are you, sir? I thought you were Ronnie Donne or I would never have let you fuck my bum in such cavalier fashion.'

'Forgive me, Miss Everleigh,' said this bright young spark. 'I know that we should first have been introduced but when I saw your glorious bottom-cheeks swaying gently from side to side as you tongued out my dear friend, I simply could not contain myself.'

'Why, come to think of it, even we two have not been formally introduced,' I said to Marie.

'Yes, you must pardon the omission,' said Marie sweetly. 'I am sure that you will have already found out that in New York we don't believe in standing upon ceremony.'

'Let us introduce ourselves now,' said the good-looking young man. 'My name is David Juckson and this is Marie

Hartland who is the manageress of my restaurant on Broadway.'

At this stage, who should come into the room but Ronnie accompanied by my own Bertie who of course had promised to pick me up when he had finished his urgent business. I blushed as Bertie stared at me for here I was stark naked on a bed with an equally nude young lady and gentleman.

I decided to brazen it out and I gave Bertie a bright greeting of welcome.

'Hello, Bertie, did you complete your affairs? As you see, I've completed mine. Still, as you Americans say, in New York you don't stand on ceremony.'

There was a brief moment of absolute silence and then we all roared with laughter as the ridiculousness of the situation dawned upon us. Ronnie and Bertie threw off their clothes and we enjoyed a grand mutual fuck with Bertie fucking me while Marie sucked off David as Ronnie pumped his enormous polehammer in and out of her eager cunt.

After washing and dressing ourselves, we walked across to David's exciting new restaurant which had, in a few short months, become one of the most fashionable new eating-houses in Manhattan. It was called the Rawalpindi and was sumptuously decorated in Eastern style. The staff were dressed in flowing gowns and the coloured head waiter was swathed in a magnificent ruby-coloured Indian dress complete with turban.

I must pause here to note on how well the art of dining is understood in New York. When the guests make their appearance, the head waiter, or *maitre d'hotel*, takes them in charge, conducts them to the table and sees them safely seated. Immediately the guests are seated, the attendant at the table brings napkins, menus and glasses of iced water, which is drunk at every meal, even in the depths of winter.

It is a peculiarity of American restaurant life that the waiter expects you to order almost everything you require at once. He may bring you soup and fish together; but he will rarely stir from your side till he learns what else you may want to complete your repast. All the substantials of the feast are thus brought at same moment. It happens of course by reason of this arrangement, that the guests find themselves surrounded by perhaps a dozen little dishes – roast beef, boiled mutton, curried chicken, potatoes, green peas, cauliflower, asparagus and a variety of other foods. Anyone who has been face to face with a 'square meal' can well understand Americans talk about 'getting through it'.

Anyhow, the head waiter gave me a menu and I studied it, though Ronnie thought our table was too near the kitchen and said so.

'Ah,' said the waiter in a rich, melodious voice. *'Ober az me zitst bay'm tepl, est men besser.'*

'Is that Urdu or Hindi?' I asked innocently. 'Obviously our waiter comes from the East.'

'East Harlem,' replied David with a smile. 'What he said was that the nearer to the pot you are, the better you eat. I trust you will enjoy our meal as I have engaged a new French chef, Monsieur Antoine Yam, directly from the Hotel Bristol in Paris. He comes highly recommended by my old friend David Lezaine, the well known international doctor and bon viveur.'

'Why, what a coincidence,' I cried 'I know Doctor Lezaine. I met him last year in London.' (Readers of the previous book in this series will remember the Belgian specialist in medicine and *amour* – Editor.)

'It's a small world, Jenny,' said Bertie, biting into one of the delicious American hot rolls that had been placed on the table.

We chatted away merrily throughout the meal. The waiters had such excellent memories that they made no mistakes in our order, however numerous the articles they were ordered to bring. And as I was to find out, if you order one or two dishes only, the waiter will frequently bring three or four, remarking as he does that he thought you had overlooked them. It is not easy to divine why everything must be placed on the table at once, even though the food is served with little gas burners underneath to keep them hot, except it be that the waiters desire to save themselves several journeys when one can answer the purpose. Anyway, the system must result in great waste for guests, not knowing the limitations of their own appetites, very often order more than they can consume.

I must add one final note, diary, on the meal. We all drank iced tea, a very agreeable American beverage prepared by pouring hot tea upon a lump of ice, mixed with sugar in a glass. Americans may drink alcoholic beverages heavily at other times, but rarely does wine make an appearance at the luncheon table. Occasionally, beer is served but, on the whole, most serious drinking occurs after sunset.

Lager beer, the common beverage, is a light and refreshing drink, and is vastly less intoxicating than the liquids consumed at home. When spirits are taken, they are usually concocted in a variety of ways. The American bartender is an artist in mixed drinks. It is a treat to observe the deftness and dexterity with which he fixes a mint julep, a sherry cobbler, a brandy smash or a gin sling.

Bertie explained to me that the saloon-keepers of New York city had a custom or organizing their customers into associations for political purposes. Each of these associations bears the name of the saloon-keeper, and the members of the society vote for any candidate in a local government election the boss chooses. The political importance of the saloon-keeper is thus assured, and he rewards his patrons with a free party every summer.

'Where publicans organize their patrons in New York, you can well imagine that social depravity goes hand in hand with political corruption,' commented Bertie sourly.

'The trouble is, we are too busy making money to bother with elections,' said our genial host, David Juckson who insisted that our sumptuous repast was 'on the house', a most generous act as the bill would have come to at least fifteen dollars. But Ronnie Donne insisted on tipping the waiters and the pretty 'hat check' girl who looks after the hats and coats of the diners while they partake of their meal. I believe he scrawled down her address for a later assignation, though David had asked all his friends not to fuck the staff because this could cause him problems. Well, perhaps the girl had a toothache!

It was time to go back to the Stuyvesant Club and to see if Molly was still feeling unwell. I hoped that she had taken the road to recovery because we had planned a very special evening which she would only enjoy if she were really fighting fit!

Fortunately, she was in the lounge when we arrived, looking quite her old self, and after Bertie took his leave she explained to me just how we planned to spend the evening.

August 7th and 8th, 1884

So, diary, what was the special evening planned by Molly and by Bertie? I had no inkling of the plan, which was devised and executed by Bertie during the morning when he pleaded 'urgent business' while I was being fucked so beautifully by Ronnie Donne, the best-hung and randiest dentist in Manhattan.

If, at that time, I had realized that dear Bertie had not deserted me but had needed the morning to make arrangements, I may well have not let the handsome Ronnie carry me off into his special recovery room!

However, I should then have deprived myself of a jolly marvellous fuck with Ronnie, and I would have known beforehand what was to happen that evening, which might have taken the gilt off the gingerbread, so to speak.

When I saw Molly at the Stuyvesant Club, she told me that we were to meet Bertie at six o'clock at the Russian Tea Rooms owned by Count Sasha Labotsky. These were situated on the corner of Fifth Avenue and 42nd Street, but we were not to dine there.

Bertie arrived punctually (a habit that I wish was more prevalent as I always do my best to be on time myself, and I hate waiting around). Then the amusements that were to follow were explained to me.

Quite simply, we were going to Ronnie Donne's home to give him a 'surprise party'. Now what makes up this genuine American institution? Well, when a family is just settling down for the evening, when the babies are in bed, when the lady of the house is just beginning to darn a hole in young Jimmy's sock, when the elder daughter has just commenced a Schubert sonata on the piano and when *Pater familias* has just settled himself in the parlour with a whisky, the house is suddenly invaded by a troupe of jovial friends.

This is the 'surprise party' and the more astonished are the 'hosts', the more appropriate is the name given to this amusement. But though the recipients are genuinely surprised, the whole expedition has been secretly organized beforehand.

It is a cardinal rule for the invaders to take with them provisions and drinks, and it is a matter of pride that all the involuntary host provides is a quantity of cutlery and glasses! As a matter of course, the quiet atmosphere of the house which has suddenly been overrun is changed to one of uproarious mirth. The fun is kept up until an advanced period of the evening, when the proceedings are brought to a close with speeches and toasts all round.

Well, to be honest, the 'surprise party' Molly and Bertie planned was just a little different from the usual sort. You see, diary, Ronnie was a bachelor who lived alone (occasionally even sleeping alone as often as once a week!) and so rather than simply play musical chairs or crowd round the piano for a sing-song, Bertie and Molly decided to hold a 'surprise sex party'.

They had rounded up several of Ronnie's friends who would shortly arrive at Count Labotsky's establishment and then we would arrive at Ronnie's all together, along with huge boxes of comestibles and crates of champagne, vodka, whisky and beer that Bertie had ordered that morning from the Count, who also provided quantities of ice at a nominal charge and promised that he himself would join the party if pressure of business allowed. Before we left he insisted that, as his guests, we sample a bowl of borscht (beetroot soup) which was absolutely delicious.

Unfortunately, David Juckson could not be with us as he had to ensure that all was well at his restaurant (a very important political personage had booked dinner for a party of no less than sixteen persons) but I was delighted to meet some more splendid people, the cream of New York's fast

45

young set to whom I was introduced. I was not to be the sole representative of Albion at the party because that well-known Berkeley Square scamp Lord Nicholas Grafton was in New York and was well acquainted with the best people in town. Bertie also brought along his cousin Graham, a tall and extremely good-looking young man whose long locks of hair were as blond as my own.

Two exquisite girls joined our group – Clara Thatcher, the daughter of the Canadian Consul-General and Hetty Hempstead, whose father had built a veritable new town over the river in the state of New Jersey. I was quite jealous of Clare's ravishing red hair which she wore in fetching ringlets, while Hetty, too, was a pretty little thing with a fine figure. She wore a low-cut gown that showed us all that she possessed an exceptionally large pair of breasts. I could see that this was already a source of attraction to Lord Nicholas, who caressed her hand for as long as he possibly could during the time that Molly and Bertie made the formal introductions.

'Now I will brook no arguments over two important matters,' said Lord Nicholas in his best imperial tone. 'Firstly, please don't address me as My Lord or Your Highness or any of that sort of rot. I answer to the name of Nicholas to my acquaintances and I am known as Nicky, or Nick Nock to my intimate friends.'

'Then it is indeed fortunate that your name is not Frederick,' chirped Molly. 'For then you might have been known as Fick Fock which would never do!'

Well, as the old saw has it, a touch of indecency makes the world laugh and this jovial remark immediately dispelled any inhibitions that members of our company might have possessed.

We drove round to Ronnie's house which was just minutes away on one of the streets that adjoins Central Park. We needed three cabs, two for our party, and one for the food and drink!

Bertie rang the bell and almost immediately a plump

Negro butler opened the door. 'Hush now, Enoch, don't give the game away!' said Bertie.

'No suh,' said the butler with a wide smile. 'This must be a surprise party, I suppose.'

'That's right,' said Bertie. 'Now where is Mr Donne?'

'He is in the drawing room, suh, looking over an article he has written for the *New England Journal of Medicine*. Do you wish me to announce you or would you like to surprise him yourself? I don't think he heard the bell.'

'We'll do it ourselves, thank you, Enoch. I wonder if you and a maid could start preparing the food and drink. I take it Mr Donne has not yet eaten?'

'Not yet, Mistuh Sand,' said Enoch. 'He only wanted a light meal as he said that he had eaten a big lunch at Mistuh Juckson's new restaurant. So cook was only going to give him some gefilte fish with red horseradish sauce.'

'I think we can do better than that,' smiled Hetty. 'But we will leave it to you and Letty to set out what we have brought in the dining room.'

'My pleasure, Miss Hempstead,' beamed the butler, holding out his arms to take our coats.

We walked as quietly as possible through the hall to the drawing-room and then Bertie flung open the door and we all yelled 'Surprise!' at the top of our voices.

Ronnie almost jumped out of his chair in astonishment. 'My God! Bertie! Molly! Clara! Good heavens, everybody's here! What on earth? Oh, my God! I know, I know! It's a surprise party!'

'That's right,' we chorused, trooping into the room. The men shook Ronnie's hand while we girls showered him with kisses.

'Don't excite him too much, girls or he won't have enough strength to play any games after supper!' warned Bertie, wagging his finger playfully at Clara and Molly.

'Oh, don't worry about that,' said Clara roguishly. 'Why, I'm told Ronnie's prick is as thick and meaty as yours, Bertie!'

'Not that she knows, of course,' said Bertie mockingly.

'Oh my, if she doesn't know now, she will certainly be able to speak from knowledge before the night is out!' said Hetty, slipping her arm inside Graham's jacket to clasp him round the waist. 'Let's go, big boy and have something to eat and drink. I'm feeling quite ravished.'

'Don't fret,' laughed Clara. 'If you're feeling ravished now, what will you be feeling after dinner, my love?'

'Well fucked, I hope,' replied Hetty sweetly as she guided Graham towards the door.

Clara smiled at Bertie who responded by taking her arm and they followed Hetty and Graham outside. It looked as if it were to be an 'all change' situation so I let Lord Nicky slip an aristocratic arm around my waist while Molly pulled Ronnie out of his chair. By the time we reached the dining room we could hear the familiar sound of champagne corks popping and we enjoyed a fine, if somewhat rowdy supper.

So we girls chose our partners for the surprise party and I must record that we feasted in fine style. Count Labotsky's genuine Russian vodka certainly led to a loosening of tongues and later, after Enoch and Letty had closed the dining room doors, a loosening of Graham's trousers by Hetty's artful fingers.

Graham was sitting on the my right-hand side and Hetty was on his right. To my amazement, the little minx was busying herself stroking the protuberance in Graham's lap and after a few moments she brazenly began to unbutton his trousers. Her fingers fumbled about inside the gap and then, with a flourish, she brought out one of the biggest pricks I have ever seen.

It stood stiffly to attention, as erect as a soldier on duty, throbbing rhythmically as Hetty licked her lips at the sight of this grand-looking tool. She moved her hands to bring out his balls in their bag of wrinkled skin and I must say that I found this scene extraordinarily exciting.

Hetty began to jerk her hand up and down the swollen shaft and Graham gurgled with delight as the touch of her soft, youthful hand sent shivers of pleasure throughout his entire frame.

Meanwhile, Lord Nicky rose to his feet and asked for quiet because he wished to dedicate a poem 'to the lovely Jenny Everleigh, the fair English rose whose beauty is unparalleled in either New York or London'.

I blushed at the compliment upon which Nicky delighted us all by announcing that he had composed a poem in my honour and that he would read it aloud to the assembled company. In a fine strong voice he declaimed:

*'Come Jenny dear! now lay your body down
Upon my naked belly white,
Now rapture soon will embraces crown,
This is the road to true delight!*

*Flowers bloom their brightest there!
Unknown fragrance fills the air.
Come sweet Jenny, grant my prayer,
Kneeling I make to thee!'*

We gave Nicky a standing ovation which was enlivened by the inevitable consequences of Hetty stimulating Graham's giant cock. For she had not let go this monster prick as he rose to applaud Nicky's poetic prowess and, indeed, had continued to rub her hand even more vigorously up and down his enormous shaft. The result was that, just as the other members of the octet had realised what was happening and had turned their eyes to gape at this public tossing off, a miniature fountain of white froth jetted out of the top of the purple bulb in a veritable arc of spunk landing directly on a plate of chocolate eclairs placed in front of our huge-cocked hero.

After a moment's stunned silence, Molly said brightly: 'Well, how kind of Graham and Hetty to give the dessert such a personal touch. I'm sure the eclairs are delicious. Bertie, please pass me the plate.'

A roar of laughter followed immediately and though Graham sat down crimson faced, no-one took the slightest offence at what had occurred. Nevertheless, our genial host had a slight criticism to make.

'I say, Graham,' drawled Ronnie. 'I think you and Hetty should entertain us properly so that we can all enjoy seeing you partaking of *l'arte de faire l'amour*.'

'Quite right, quite right!' called out Clara. 'I dare you two to fuck on the carpet in front of us!'

'Now you know that I can never resist a challenge,' said Hetty, her hand still busy with Graham's cock, slipping his foreskin over and under the glistening dome on which there were still a few dribbles of sperm.

'But can Graham come again?' I asked.

'A hard man is good to find,' said Ronnie Donne.

'I think I can perform adequately enough,' said Graham, removing Hetty's hand from his still semi-erect cock. He proceeded to take off the remainder of his clothes to the cheers of the assembly and I write without shame that the sight of his superb manly frame sent the blood coursing through my veins in a frenzy of sensual excitement.

His shoulders were so broad and his deep chest was lightly covered with fine light brown hair and the swell of his dimpled buttocks raised my appetite for a fuck even further. But, meanwhile, all I could do was to admire from afar that monstrous staff which was almost back to its former thickness and truncheon-like hardness and which lucky Hetty could now cajole up to the peak of perfection.

Hetty quickly disrobed and a murmur of appreciation ran through the room as we gazed at her nude charms. She was a truly lovely girl. Her somewhat dark-skinned oval face was set off prettily by a mop of light brown hair, a pair of large, merry hazel-coloured eyes and a generous mouth. But her best attributes were undoubtedly the snowy prominences of her large bosoms. What exquisitely firm breasts were exposed to our admiring view and it was no wonder that Graham immediately placed his hands on those rosy red nipples that stood out sharply even before he tweaked them up to full hardness.

Her soft, white belly was bared to our eyes and I noted a finely chiselled crack with red pouting lips only semi-hidden by the luxuriant growth of silky black hair between her legs.

Graham took all the liberties he desired with this gorgeous girl, kissing and sucking her pretty lips, the nipples of her firm breasts, handling her bum cheeks and frigging her erect little clitoris as she writhed in delight upon the shaggy cream carpet. He drew up his monster cock between her thighs and rubbed her pussy lips as she moaned in sheer pleasure, hugging him in her arms, giving kiss for kiss, grappling for the ruby head of his prick which she wanted between the yearning lips of her cunney.

They sank to the carpet and she twisted round to make Graham lie on his back whilst she rode a magnificent St George upon him. We could see his mighty cock standing stiff as a flagpole as she rose up and down deliberately upon it. As her cunney opened up to receive this throbbing member, her juices began to flow copiously and the slick squish of their mating was extraordinarily arousing, not only for me, but to other members of the distinguished party.

Ronnie went to a sideboard and produced a large white towel. 'Here,' he called, 'I'm laying out this towel for you two and any others who might follow as this carpet cost me two thousand dollars and I don't want it ruined by spunk and cunt juice!'

The obliging pair rolled over to continue their performance on Ronnie's towel. Hetty was now on her back and her legs were wrapped around Graham's waist as he pumped his willing cock in and out of her juicy cunney. This was too exciting a situation for young Lord Nicky who in a trice had removed his clothes and who now stood stark naked rubbing his well-sized cock which rose up majestically against his slim belly.

Hetty caught sight of this fine prick and took hold of it, slipping his foreskin behind the mushroom dome which she guided between her lips, slurping uninhibitedly as she sucked the swollen shaft.

This wild girl now motioned to Graham to revert to their previous position which they accomplished without his cock losing its place between her pouting cunney lips. Now as she bounced up and down his hard truncheon she suddenly took Nicky's cock out of her mouth and whispered, 'Go behind, darling.'

Nicky needed no further command, so kneeling behind her he tried to insert his prick in her cunt to share that happy haven with Graham but this was impossible to achieve. Then the charming crinkled orifice of her pink bottom-hole caught his attention and as the tip of his cock was already wet from its luscious sucking, his vigorous shoves soon gained an entrance into this tighter hole.

Hetty found the sensation of enjoying two cocks at once somewhat too exciting and asked them to rest for a few moments. This they did and they too clearly enjoyed the sensation of feeling where they were, their pricks throbbing against each other in a most delicious manner, with only the thin membrane of the anal canal between them.

This exquisite feeling led to the two boys spending quickly once they resumed their fucking of Hetty, who gave a great scream as she received two libations of hot spunk simultaneously in her cunt and her arsehole.

Spontaneously we broke into applause as the boys rolled off Hetty, one on each side, and she grasped a cock in each hand to shake out the last drops of frothy spunk from her gallant lovers.

'Gad, that was a marvellous fuck,' panted Nicky. 'You New York girls certainly know how to fuck.'

'Hey, what's wrong with home-grown cunney?' laughed Molly.

'Nothing at all, my love, except that there just don't seem to be so many English girls around who know how to enjoy themselves when making love,' he rejoined.

'Is that so? I'll show you how good we are at fucking.

Now, I bet I can get your cock stiff in minutes even though you have just shot your bolt with Hetty.'

'I don't think so,' said Nicky doubtfully.

'I bet I can!' said Molly, with no little confidence.

'No, I don't think I am up to it – in every sense of the phrase!'

'I'll bet fifty dollars Molly can have his cock sky high in three minutes,' Ronnie Donne interjected. 'Have I any takers?'

'You're on,' said Bertie. 'Here, Jenny, you hold the stakes.'

As Molly stripped down to total nudity, the boys each handed me a fifty dollar bill. 'I'll be the timekeeper!' piped up Clara, and Graham handed her his silver watch and chain. 'Are you ready, Molly? OK, the clock is starting in five seconds, five, four, three, two, one, go!'

Molly dropped down to the towel and proceeded to turn Hetty over on her tummy so as to expose her lovely tight little arse cheeks to our lascivious gaze.

'Now then, Hetty,' she said severely. 'You have been a naughty girl, having cocks in your cunt and your bum at the same time. And you know what happens to naughty girls, don't you? They get their bottoms smacked!'

And she sat down and pulled Hetty over her knees, at first caressing the superbly proportioned bum cheeks and slipping her hand between them to bring out the juices from her still wet cunney.

Then she began to smack Hetty's beautiful bum, lightly but with rapid little slaps which must have made her bottom tingle as the skin turned rapidly from creamy white to pink.

'Oooh! Oooh! Molly! Oh, no more, oh no, I beg of you, ow!, ow!, ow!'

But Molly took no notice as she continued to administer the punishment.

'Quiet now, Hetty!' she snapped. 'You have been a bad girl and your deserve a slapping. Besides, I like to see the way the flesh of your bottom changes colour. Bright pink suits you and anyway I love the way your bum cheeks jiggle as I slap them!'

Sure enough, after just one minute, thirty seven seconds (as Clara later informed us), Nicky's cock was rock hard and he was on his knees next to Molly who, without missing one beat of her rhythm as she smacked Hetty's tingling bottom, clamped her full red lips around his rampant cock.

Mercifully for Hetty's poor bum, Molly now ceased her spanking and circled her hands around Nicky's pulsating prick, which already had a blob of milky white froth at the end of his knob. She jammed down the foreskin and lashed her tongue round the shaft, slurping with great gusto. Meanwhile, Hetty had raised herself on her hands and knees and, lowering her pretty little head, began to kiss and suck Hetty's bush with equal vigour and we saw her pink tongue flash in and out of Molly's quim.

It was now Bertie's turn to slip quickly out of his clothes and position himself behind Hetty whose rounded bum cheeks, still slightly pink from Molly's ministrations, were moving in rhythm as she sucked on Molly's dripping cunney. Ever game, Hetty took hold of Bertie's sturdy member with her right hand and directed its rich red ruby head to the glorious cheeks of her bum.

Hetty stopped licking out Molly's cunt for a moment to say: 'Don't fuck my arsehole, Bertie, it'll get very sore. But do fuck my cunt from behind. I would enjoy that immensely.'

Bertie was nothing loath and, as Hetty bent down to continue tonguing Molly's cunney, she pushed out her bum and opened her legs to allow him access. Carefully, Bertie positioned the tip of his cock between her cunney lips and he began to move first in easy rhythm and then faster and faster like a jockey at Ascot races. At the same time, Hetty increased the tempo of her licking Molly's cunney and Molly quickened the pace of the sucking of Nicky's cock, delicately flicking her tongue along the shaft.

Nicky was the first to explode, his prick twitching uncontrollably as Molly gently squeezed his balls. Quickly, she jammed her mouth over his knob and greedily gulped down the thick jets of spunk that gushed out of his cock into her throat.

Now her own orgasm began to flow and love-juice poured out from her hairy bush into Hetty's willing mouth who sucked hard to drain all the liquor pouring out of Molly's cunt.

Moments later, it was Bertie's turn, as Hetty's bottom responded to every shove and thrust of his lusty cock. The contractions of her cunt sucked the seed from his shaft and the sweet friction of her cunney lips against the head of his prick made every nerve thrill with pleasure as he flooded her womb with hot spurts of spunk. Oh, the four of them made up a truly wonderful picture of voluptuous pleasure.

So far, Ronnie, Clara and I had stood on the sidelines but now we decided to join in the fun in earnest and within a very short space of time, all eight of us young people were locked in a marvellous naked embrace.

Although I desperately needed a good stiff cock inside me, I found myself caressing the lovely redheaded Clara whose auburn locks I so admired.

Clara was slight with a feline grace in her figure and face that was very tempting. Her face was well proportioned, with glorious light brown eyes, and her abundance of cascading curls of auburn hair made her a ravishing girl.

Without words, we exchanged kisses and my mouth descended lower. I ran over each snowy white breast in turn, flicking and chewing quickly on each engorged nipple that ornamented each lovely globe. My hand slipped down to the silky bush of auburn hair between her thighs and I inserted a deft finger into her moist, yet tight, little pussey as she wriggled and cooed with joy.

Now she was on her back with her long legs stretched wide apart, inviting me to bury my face between them. I parted her soft, lightly scented pubic mound with my fingertips to reveal her swollen clitty. As I worked my face into the cleft between her thighs, I could not help but notice how clean and appetising her pussey looked.

By this time, I was down on my tummy, between her legs with one hand under her bottom for a little elevation and the other reaching around her thigh so I could spread her cunney lips with my thumb and middle finger. Her juices were already dribbling like honey from her parted labia, and her clitoris turned from pale pink to deep red as I flicked gently with the wet edge of my darting tongue.

I placed my lips over her clitty and first nibbled daintily away at it and then I sucked it firmly up into my mouth, where the tip of my tongue began to explore it from all directions. I could feel it growing erect as Clara's legs wriggled and twitched up and down along the side of my own body.

Then I found the little button under the fold at the base of her clitty and began to start twirling my tongue around it. As I moved it up and down, she became more and more excited and I was forced to grasp her bum cheeks to maintain my hold on her clitty. The faster I vibrated her clitty, the quicker she began to gyrate, moaning loudly and rocking her head from side to side as the juices began to flow out of her.

Our bodies were stretched to their supple limits and I was tempted to suck her even harder and pushing my mouth hard up against her, I began to move my entire head back and forth. Oh, how wet she was! Her head was thrown back now, her shoulders shaking as little quakes ran through her body while my tongue moved even more quickly along the silken groove of her cunt, licking and lapping her delicious juices that ran down like a stream, mixing with my own saliva.

Her pussey was now gushing love juice and each time I tongued her I felt Clara's clitty stiffen perceptibly, even more eager and pulsating, wanting more and more until with a little scream she exploded into a marvellous, all-embracing orgasm.

Our performance as tribades excited all the four men who stood around us, their cocks standing high with excitement. Hetty and Molly joined us and we each chose a prick to suck. I decided to taste Graham's monster cock and I had to use both hands to guide the thick shaft into my mouth. On my left, Molly was sucking noisily away on Ronnie's fine tool, while on my right Clara was engaged in licking Bertie's thick prick. Meanwhile Hetty was busy gobbling Lord Nicky's smooth shafted prick.

I gently stroked the underside of this huge cock, allowing my fingers to trace a path around and underneath his equally huge balls until I felt his prick was at its peak height. I could not take in more than two and a half inches of this great shaft as the thickness of his prick would not allow more; my excitement grew stronger and stronger and I was frightened that he would squirt off in my mouth.

Now I enjoy the taste of spunk but I wanted that extraordinary cock in my cunt so I gently extracted his cock from my mouth and lay down on the carpet, spreading my legs so that he was afforded a good view of my juicy quim. Graham kissed me. His lips were very wet and soft and I could feel his tongue exploring every last inch of my mouth. He then moved down between my legs and put his mouth on my titties, sucking and nibbling each in turn until I shuddered with anticipation. I closed my eyes as I felt his huge pole nudging between my legs.

He kissed me again, then with a swift, strong stroke he entered me; then again, deeper and harder as my body arched and Graham's tongue moved in and out of my mouth in perfect unison with his cock as I writhed in ecstasy. As he gripped me more tightly and tensed his body against mine, I gasped as my body prepared to erupt. His prick began throbbing against my cunney walls and at the exact second he thrust in and pumped great wads of spunk inside me, I too reached orgasm in a shivering, quivering, joyous, mutual climax.

We were now all in need of a rest, but after only a short

while I had the need to participate in a further round of activities. I decided to approach Graham because I felt that this big man was of a stronger constitution than the others.

I was not to be disappointed. We began with some kisses and cuddles and then laying me down on the carpet he began to kiss me all over. We both squirmed about until I found myself kneeling between his thighs. It was only natural that in that position I took his cock in both hands, taking the hot tip between my lips and sucking in its juicy sponginess while releasing one hand to squeeze his balls. I flicked my tongue under the swollen helmet and, bobbing my head in a deliberately slow tempo, I began to fuck Graham with my suctioning mouth.

Oh, I did enjoy having his stiff, pulsating prick rising high just in front of my drooling mouth. I reached up and guided as much of his massive prick as I could into my mouth, licking and nibbling at the swollen head. I lifted my mouth from his cock for an instant to draw in a lungful of air, only to expel it as a rapturous moan due to the lustful fever burning in my body.

I continued to suck this magnificent naked cock and I could feel little squirts of spunk coming into my mouth which I hastily swallowed as I knew that the big gush could not be far behind. I grasped the lean cheeks of his bottom as I moved him backwards and forwards as he held my head firmly to give maximum penetration.

Suddenly he called out: 'I'm going to spend, Jenny, Suck me! Fuck! Ohhh . . .!' His hips began to move, faster, thrusting, pumping his iron hard prick in and out of my mouth as with tightly compressed lips, I held his shaft tightly inside me.

His cock swelled and I felt it throb and then a hot stream of sperm spurted into my eager mouth and flowed down my willing throat. I have always enjoyed the invigorating, salty taste of spunk and I gulped down Graham's copious emission with great delight. I licked up every last drain of spunk, running my pink tongue all over his knob and across the little 'eye' to scoop up any remaining droplet.

Now it was my turn to lie back, spread my legs and wait to be pleasured by Graham's darting tongue. He placed his handsome head against my silky blonde mound and without ado began to lick my pussey lips which he parted with his hand.

He sat up for a moment and leaned back, his mouth sticky from where he had been kissing my pussey and said: 'What a delicious cunt you have, Jenny; it smells so sweet and has such thick full lips. Yet though so large, the entrance itself is as tight as possible and will no doubt fit my cock like a glove when I introduce him to you. But first I shall give your cunt the most exquisite licking which I trust will produce the feelings of bliss I was delighted to experience while you were sucking my cock.'

'Action, not words! Finish me off with your tongue, darling!' I pleaded, and being a true Yankee, Graham bent forward again, his lips nuzzling against my cunney lips, teasing his tongue between them until I screamed out with pleasure.

He found my clitty and kept up a nice steady rhythm of the most salacious sucking. It must have been telepathy but he knew just the right time to withdraw his hand and tongue and replace them by the uncovered ruby-red head of his huge cock which nudged between my pussey lips. I was already so wet that I could feel my own love juice dribbling down my thighs and though Graham inserted at least six inches of his monster cock inside me, he was so gentle that I felt no pain at all, just an overwhelming fullness.

Each push filled me with even more cock until I could feel his large balls bang against my bum as I lifted my legs to wrap around his waist. He slid in and then almost out of me with each thrust with my buttocks heaving up to meet his thrusts, my arms clinging convulsively round his body.

Another climax was building up inside me and he must have sensed this too as he started to change his long strokes into short stabbing thrusts. He held me tightly to him and I felt his cock pulsating and jerking deep inside my love-channel. We came together in a luscious spend, waves of orgasms rippling through my cunt as, with an exclamation of rapture, Graham sent a boiling gush of frothy spunk crashing through my already lubricated cunney. I shall never forget the sight of that beautiful red-headed cock as it stood out in all its manly glory, stiff and hard as marble with the hot spunk threatening to burst from the thick knob that capped the lovely shaft!

Graham and I were now truly *hors de combat* so my lover found some cushions upon which we lay quite nude, drinking some ice-cold champagne whilst Molly and Clara nuzzled up to Ronnie Donne, their two tongues lashing his semi-hard cock up to full erection. But clever little Hetty took advantage of their labours – and the total nakedness of the company – to sit on Ronnie's stiff truncheon, her cuntal lips engorging his pole which slid up her as her soft folds enveloped his shaft. She rode a superb St George upon Ronnie, leaning forward so he could knead her perfectly moulded breasts and rub his palm across her erect little red titties. Her tight cunney seemed to suck upon his embedded cock, imploring it to throb and slide inside its slippery haven as she bounced happily away up and down upon her pole.

Molly and Clara were sporting enough to let Hetty ride without interference, although she had jumped the queue. But the girls wanted Ronnie for themselves so to shorten Hetty's ride, Molly gently squeezed Ronnie's balls. He cried out as his climax quickened and in moments he was pumping thick wodges of white spunk as Hetty cried out 'Ronnie! Ronnie! Oh fill me, yes! What floods!' The rich juice from his balls continued to pump out in great leaping jets as groaning, he made a final effort to eject the final spurts and then collapsed on his back, quite exhausted from this short but intensely enjoyable little fuck.

The evening continued in such delicious license. As with all surprise parties, the fun is kept up till an advanced period of the evening. When the clocks struck midnight, we all hurriedly dressed ourselves and brought the proceedings to a close in the usual manner. Bertie took it upon himself to deliver the speech in honour of the host on behalf of the guests whilst Ronnie replied in equally complimentary terms about his unexpected visitors. We returned back to the club after bidding the gentlemen goodnight, delighted with the success of the evening's entertainment.

Often a surprise party furnishes a subject for gossip and, in rural areas, even paragraphs in the local newspapers. But at this party the guests were few and selectively chosen for their discretion as well as their manifest physical attributes. Indeed, we all realised that discretion was vital for the merest whiff of scandal would ruin the chance of any further such gatherings.

I looked at Molly as she undressed. She looked bright and cheerful though the hour was late and we had eaten and drunk and fucked for several hours. I, too, felt a warm, pleasant glow coursing through my frame. There can be little doubt, dear diary, that a girl who is well and frequently fucked may be seen through her healthy complexion and general merriness to be so. That is not to say that she is open to all in her favours. Indeed, *au contraire*, she must choose her sexual partners with care, cloaking herself where needs be in an exclusivity that can be unwound at will.

Although I have let my high sensuality occasionally lead me to an occasional indiscreet fuck, on the whole I have chosen well. Never has the hand of expulsion been raised to me or any of my like-minded friends. Mind you, dear diary, it is also true that most tongues know better than to wag lest others wag back at them!

I must close this epistle because tomorrow Graham and Bertie have invited Molly and I to spend some days out of New York. Our first stop will be Washington and I am looking forward eagerly to visiting the capital of the Republic.

August 14th, 1887

Nothing in America appeared to me so much superior to what we have in Great Britain as the system of railway travelling. I must add here that the Americans have adopted the term railroad instead of railway. It is a real comfort to travel in America compared to the weary, dreary business that it is in England.

What more than anything else conducive to comfort in America is the construction of the carriages which are universally known here as cars. British carriages are low, cold, draughty and ill-ventilated, while American cars are far better constructed.

A platform at each end furnishes access to what is really a long, lofty and handsome apartment. Seats for two persons are ranged on each side and these seats are reversible so that the members of a party travelling together can face each other if they so wish. Tables in some cases are fixed between the seats and the windows can be opened and shut with ease and are fitted with venetian blinds in such a way that the direct rays of the sun can be excluded. The lofty roofs of the cars provide for good ventilation, while to persons familiar with the dim lights supplied on our British railways, the bright and cheerful illumination of an American car must be suprising. Handsome chandeliers hang from the ceiling – some of them supplied with oil, others with gas and others again, as in our special Pullman car, with electricity!

Iced water is provided in each car and it is perhaps not so well known that in general there is only one class of travel – not three as in England. There are particular cars reserved for ladies and children on many trains, while for long journeys Pullman, Wagner and Woodruff sleeping and parlour cars are provided for those wealthy travellers who want extra comforts.

The arrangements connected with these magnificent conveyances are so ingenious that travelling in them is a genuine luxury. I will not bore you, dear diary, with all the details, but suffice it to note that the reclining chairs are covered with red velvet and are so constructed in combination with rests for the feet that the passenger can adjust them to eight different positions. Hence, when tired of sitting, one can if one pleases, compose oneself for a nap as comfortably as on the sofa in one's own house.

Anyway, the four of us, Graham and Bertie, Molly and I left Grand Central Station in New York early in the morning. Graham and Bertie, the American cousins, had booked a private compartment on a Pullman car for the English cousins, Molly and I. We left our seats to walk through to the dining car and I must digress again, diary, to note the varied and wholesome breakfast we enjoyed for only eighty five cents per person. Here is the 'breakfast bill of fare' from which we chose our *petit déjeuner*:

Fruits
Apples   Strawberries   Oranges

Drinks
English Breakfast Tea   Coffee   Iced Milk   Chocolate

Bread
French Loaf   Boston Brown Bread   Corn Bread
Hot Rolls   Buttered Toast

Fish
Whitefish Broiled

Broiled
Tenderloin Steak, plain or with Mushrooms
Mutton Chops   Spring Chicken   Sugar Cured Ham

Cold Dishes
Pressed Corned Beef   Ham   Tongue

Eggs
Omelettes   Boiled   Scrambled   Fried

Potatoes
Baked   Stewed   Fried

Miscellaneous
Calf's Liver with Bacon   Oat Meal   Breakfast Bacon

Relishes
Chow Chow   Currant Jelly   Worcestershire Sauce
Mixed Pickles   Horseradish

We returned to our private quarters and Molly and I enjoyed looking out of the window at the lovely scenery, while the boys busied themselves with the study of the newspapers which we had purchased before we left. Actually, we need not have bothered for newsboys actually ride on main city services. The first time he pays the passengers a visit he brings round a stock of newpapers and, soon afterwards an armful of magazines, books and postcards.

The light was shining rather brightly in the compartment so Graham adjusted the venetian blinds for me.

'That was a delicious breakfast,' chirped Molly.

'Yes, I am so full, I just want to have a snooze,' I said.

'Oh, come now Jenny,' cried Bertie. 'Have you never enjoyed the thrill of fucking on a train? It is a long journey to Washington and I can think of nothing better to pass the time than threading my cock into your juicy warm cunt!'

Readers of my earlier diaries will know of my escapade with Johnny Oaklands on a train from the West Country to Paddington but I refrained from imparting this knowledge to Molly and the boys.

'I am sure we do no such thing in stuffy old England,' said Molly with a giggle.

Graham, who will you remember was a bibliophile, interrupted her to say: 'You must forgive me, Molly, but you most certainly do. Have you never come across *"The Secret Journals of Colonel Lionel Moore M C D S O"*? He claims to have participated in perhaps the first railway fucking ever to take place. It was just over fifty years ago on the famous occasion that the English politician Huskisson became the first person to be killed by a railway engine, George Stephenson's Rocket.

'What few people know is that at the very moment that poor Huskisson was mortally wounded, Colonel Moore's cock was penetrating a luscious wet cunney in his private carriage. The girl had been jammed into one of the wretched third class trucks with no roof and had been drenched in a rainstorm. The gallant Colonel invited her into his domain to dry off. After she had taken off her wet clothes the Colonel pulled out his prick and hey presto!

'Indeed, the Colonel became so enamoured of fucking in a train that he consummated his marriage to Lady Elizabeth Thomson-Jones on the Scotch Express,' added Graham earnestly.

'Well, I'm game,' Molly declared. 'How about you, Jenny?'

'I really am a little tired,' I said truthfully. 'Why don't you and the boys begin the proceedings and if I feel like it – which I probably will – I shall join you in the frolics a little later.'

Bertie moved across to sit beside me as Graham and Molly exchanged a warm embrace. 'Oh, you are a lovely boy,' cooed Molly as they kissed. 'Your teeth are lovely and white and your body looks so firm and strong.'

Emboldened by her eagerness, Graham worked his hands inside the bosom of her dress and Molly eased the passage by undoing the buttons of her blouse. Now her tongue was in his mouth and as she shucked off her dress, I could see Graham's fingers tickling her large titties, that were already sticking out as stiff as little cocks. 'Aaaaah!' whispered Molly, as Graham ran his free hand down her belly and smoothed his palm over the inviting, moist blonde bush of cunney hair. He began to frig her gently with his forefinger and Molly wriggled under this double excitement of tittie and cunney. Her hands groped outside his trousers to unfasten the buttons and bring out the bursting prick inside them. One by one she delicately undid his fly and then her soft delicate hand had possession of Graham's monster cock, naked and palpitating with unslaked desire.

He pulled off his trousers and Molly said she would like to ride a St George on his huge cock. So Graham sat back on his chair, naked from the waist down, his great prick standing upright from between his legs as he pulled Molly over him as tenderly as he knew how, running his hands over her deliciously rounded breasts. She, always all readiness, guided his magnificent cock, not without a little difficulty into her moist little cunt. She wriggled delighedly for some moments and then with a cry, flung herself up and down with some violence upon his vibrating prick, uttering little cries of joy. Her legs were clamped in a vice-like grip around his and from the closed eyes and expression of sheer joy on Graham's face, I knew that Molly's clever cunt muscles were working their magic.

'Oh yes! Oh lovely! Oh, yes you big-cocked boy, let it go and fill me up with your hot juice!' shouted Molly.

Nothing loath, with one enormous thrust of the hips, Graham rammed his giant cock into her to its fullest extent. Molly shrieked with delight as he spunked inside her, filling her womb with fuck-fluid, rhythmically contracting her juicy cunney to drain that fine cock of all its jism. Molly, too, spent copiously as they swam in a sea of pleasure.

This excellent exhibition of *l'arte de faire I l'amour* had almost unconsciously stimulated my appetite for I looked down to find that I had unbuttoned Bertie's trousers and taken out his naked cock and had pleasured us both by rubbing the splendid shaft, capping and uncapping the red-headed knob, bringing it to a fine state of erection.

'Suck me off, please, Jenny,' said Bertie and I was happy to oblige. I sank down on the floor between his legs still caressing his thick cock. I kissed the ruby knob and then opened my lips to take it in my mouth. I sucked gently, rolling my tongue over it and then began to suck fully on his gorgeous, tasty cock. My tongue ran down the length of the shaft and ran back to the dome to catch a sticky drip of spend that had formed round the 'eye'. I ran my lips round that noble cock, closing my lips round the sweetmeat, sucking greedily as I squeezed his balls carefully to heighten his enjoyment.

Soon Bertie orgasmed, sending a jet of lovely creamy spunk down my throat in a frenzy of salty froth which I swallowed to the final burning drops, squeezing his balls to milk his cock of every last drain.

We undressed fully now and Bertie took me in his strong arms, laying me down on the soft carpet. We kissed each other with tender deep thrusts of our tongues in each other's mouths and I felt his prick swell against my pussey bush. I may have sucked out all his spend but Bertie was a healthy young man in his prime. In no time at all, his thick prick was again standing fully erect, pressing down hard against my belly.

Bertie then slightly raised himself on to his hands and then thrust his diamond-hard rod firmly into my juicy pussey. The lunge and thrust was nigh perfect and my cunt seemed to burst open like a water lily as the fiery red monster plunged into me, our hairy matted triangles mingling as he pumped that fine tool in and out of my soaking snatch. The lips of my cunney parted before his onslaught, wet and willing as I rocked beneath him.

My hungry cunt, with what eagerness it sucked in so delicious a morsel! Oh! There is truly nothing to be compared to a stiff cock for gratifying a girl who knows and understands the supreme delights of fucking.

I grasped his firm bum-cheeks, vigorously heaving up to meet each thust he gave, gasping out: 'Dear Bertie, oh, push it in, drive it home, Aaaah! That's the way! Oh, Bertie how your lovely prick fills my cunt. Fuck me hard, fuck me fast!'

His rampant cock pumped up and down at a steady pace

until he sensed by my shuddering that I was ready to climb to the highest points of excitement. He then increased the tempo of his jerking cock until I was almost frantic with lust. 'Oh, yes! yes! yes! Shoot your spunk into me now!' I screamed out, caring nothing that my voice might be heard by passengers in the next compartment. Almost before the words were out of my mouth, Bertie shot a heavy load of creamy white love cream into me as our pubic mounds crashed together. We writhed happily on the carpet as my hips gyrated forwards and backwards to enclose every inch of that superb shaft that had so lovingly driven me to such heights of ecstacy.

We lay panting, totally exhausted from this splendid fuck when the possible happening which had briefly crossed my mind a moment before – namely that our cries of passion would be overheard-became actual reality. The door of the compartment (which we had foolishly left unlocked) flew open and a tall bulky man stood in the entrance.

'Oh, my apologies,' he said as his dark eyes swept across the compartment, taking in the sight of two naked young men and two equally nude young girls sprawled out on the seats.

Speaking with a slight European accent, he continued: 'You must forgive the intrusion but I heard noises coming from this compartment and I assumed quite wrongly that I may have been needed.'

I looked at the figure in the doorway and he returned my stare. Then together our memories stirred with a mutual recognition. 'Jenny Everleigh, it is you, is it not?' he smiled. 'I wonder if you remember me?'

'I most certainly do,' I replied. 'It is Doctor David Lezaine, unless I am very much mistaken.'

'No, no, you are quite correct. It must be some three years since we last met. As I recall, it was at Victoria Station in London. You were with my friend Monsieur Harold Le Meshigunah when I arrived from Paris to give a talk at University College.'

'That's right, you looked at my dear friend Johnny Oakland's penis for he was worried about a small wart that had appeared on the shaft,' I said.

'What a memory you possess! Yes, and I examined his prick and was able to tell him that this was a totally benign penile wart and that there was nothing to worry about. If only all young men would be so sensible and go to their doctors if they have any worries about their cocks. In the vast majority of cases, there is absolutely nothing to worry about and their minds are eased. And if, in the minority of cases, there is some form of disease, well, the sooner it is treated, the better the chance of a complete recovery and the lessening of the chance of passing on an infection. H'm, looking at these two lucky young men, I hope they have no need of my services!'

'Ah,' I said. 'Let me introduce you. Doctor David Lezaine, a great medical specialist from Belgium, this is my cousin Molly, and the two gentlemen are Graham and Bertie Sand.'

'Delighted to meet you,' said the genial doctor. 'Oh, please do not get dressed on my account. Especially you, Molly, what a fine pair of breasts you have. And what a silky blonde bush! I see many nude women in the course of my work but the sight of a beautiful naked girl still arouses my passions!'

'Well, do come in and join us,' said the ever-hospitable Molly. 'Shut the door and this time we will lock it so we shall not be interrupted. The only thing now, dear doctor, is that you are dressed and the rest of us are undressed which is not a satisfactory state of affairs.'

'Indeed it is not,' laughed Doctor Lezaine. 'I shall quickly rectify that situation. But please, let us not stand upon ceremony, particularly here in this marvellously exciting new country. Do call me David as do all my friends.'

He quickly disrobed exhibiting a fine, broad chest covered with dark hair and a belly quite flat for a man of his years – I suppose he must have been in his forties – with a powerful-looking cock which Molly immediately grasped as they sat down together. David was obviously taken with Molly's undoubted beauty – her beautiful full breasts were as firm and as round as two globes whilst the mass of silky blonde hair between her thighs contrasted exquisitely with the snowy whiteness of her belly. David was a lucky man as his introduction to Molly came at a time when her blood was up and she was feeling very aroused. She did not make a habit of fucking with all and sundry, I must add, but once she had been formally introduced and she knew that the man was a gentleman, well, why waste time with all the boring preliminaries? Usually, however, she would have wished to be wooed but, as I say, this was somewhat of an unusual occasion.

In an inkling they were entwined on the long seat as I made room for them, taking my place between Graham and Bertie. David's head immediately ducked down between her thighs as Molly opened her legs wide. His strong arms lifted her hips and we saw his tongue flick out to thrust between the pouting lips of her cunt. Her bottom cheeks, both clutched in his firm hands, began a merry dance as he lapped at her pussey in slow yet persistent strokes, kissing and sucking her cunney, mingling his saliva with her love juice which was already beginning to flow.

She slid her fingers over her breasts, clutching and pinching her titties as she grasped: 'Oh! Oh! I am going to spend! Yes! Yes! There! Oh, my that is so delicious!' Her creamy emission flowed over David's tongue which now rested as she added: 'Oh, David! You are truly an expert muff-diver. Now let me suck your cock before you put it in my cunney.'

He groaned with passion for no sooner had she uttered these words than she slid across, keeping herself sufficiently well-placed for David to continue lapping at her erect little clitty, and took the bulbous head between her soft warm, lips. Feeling the gorgeous grasp of her red lips about his cock, David's back arched in ecstasy.

'Suck! Suck! Suck, *ma cherie!*' he cried hoarsely, pushing

her head down as she absorbed another three inches of prick in her mouth. But Molly was concerned that he would spend too quickly, so abandoning her delicious sweetmeat, she cast herself on her back, her legs wide apart, showing her pouting cunney lips to great effect. 'Come, David, stick your cock in me; let's fuck!'

His cock waggling in anticipation David climbed upon her rich curves immediately. A satisfied 'Aaaah!' from both signalled that he had met his target in an instant and parting softly to his first push, we saw his shaft slip sweetly in between the velvet lips. Their lips met in the most passionate of kisses and Molly jerked her bum petulantly, the quicker to absorb him. With a choking cry of bliss, he thrust every inch of his not inconsiderable shaft inside her, while his balls crashed against her bottom. And there the couple lay enlaced and still for a moment, but then Molly panted: 'Come on, now David, give me a good fucking!'

'Ah, yes, ma cherie. Ah! How luscious and tight your slit is, how glorious your bum-cheeks and your titties, how rosy and how firm they jut out. I must suck them!'

'Oh! Keep thrusting! Ah, what a lovely prick you have! Faster, faster, I know you have spunk boiling in your balls for me, darling!'

'That I have! Work your hips, make me spend, listen to the squelch of our juices!'

Now quite berserk, the couple thrust and moaned as David's cock slewed joyously in and out of its slick haven. 'Now, David, now!' yelled Molly and he obeyed almost instantly, flooding her cunney with such vibrant shoots of spunk that Molly arched her back and we could see the ripples of orgasmic joy that ran down her spine as she shuddered to a delightful climax. As she artfully wiggled her bum cheeks, spout after spout of creamy foam filled her cunney until David withdrew his glistening shaft and sank back on his haunches as the delightful spendings melted away to a tiny drop of white sperm on the top of his knob.

Almost unconsciously, I had taken hold of the two cocks

on either side of me and Bertie and Graham both grunted with pleasure as I rubbed them both up to a mutual climax, leaving my hands coated with spunk as fountains of cream gushed up from my two fine lovers.

We continued our journey in the same fashion. As my old friend Sir Godfrey Hendon used to say: 'A good fuck really sets you up for the day'. And truth to tell, the American countryside is rather boring. There is an absence of hedge-rows, which are the glory of our own little island, and the strict geographical formation of the agricultural holdings makes for monotony. Doctor Johnson used to say that one field was like another to him – if he had seen one, he had seen all. Had the crusty old doctor ever travelled in America, he would have had more right to dogmatize in this fashion. For here the fields (if they may be so called) are nearly all of one pattern.

A series of oblong shapes, divided by rail fences of the roughest and most commonplace character, and disfigured here and there by the stumps of half-burnt trees, constitute a large part of American rural scenery. Without that wealth of hawthorn and blackthorn, or that diversity of shape in the divisions of property which makes our English scenery so pleasant to the eye, the American landscape (except where hills or forest lend enchantment to the view) frequently palls upon the fancy.

In fairness, though, I must mention the reverse side to this coin; British farmhouses are for the most part, destitute of attractive qualities. But the houses in the rural areas of America, invariably constructed of wood and almost always painted in bright, cheerful colours, are very pleasing.

Be that as it may, when we heard the conductor call out that in thirty minutes time we would be in Washington, we quickly dressed ourselves, though Molly insisted on sucking off Doctor Lezaine, whose mighty cock was still standing high. He repaid the compliment by finger-fucking my dear cousin from behind as she knelt on the seat besides him.

Bertie and Graham had arranged a meeting with Senator

Jonathan Easthouse and the Senator's own carriage was waiting at the terminus for us. We bade our farewells to Doctor Lezaine who insisted that we joined him later that evening at his club, the Beesknees, which was affiliated, as I later found out, to the Jim-Jam in London. And readers of my earlier diaries will know what the speciality of that establishment happened to be!

Now I must record my impressions of Washington, dear diary, even though my pussey is aching somewhat from the exercise of last night at the Beesknees which I will recount a little later.

The capital of the Republic is not unworthy of this great and prosperous nation. Washington is an absolute creation of the Federal Congress. Other cities have grown but Washington was made. The site chosen for the seat of government was well adapted for the purpose, though some of the lower ground is said to be conducive to malaria.

Large ideas pervaded the founders of the city who provided for a development commensurate with the development of the United States. Hence, they placed the public departments so far away from one another that Washington became happily designated the City of Magnificent Distances. The distances are still magnificent, but the intervening spaces have now almost all been filled up with handsome residences. Yet the streets and avenues remain broad, all planted with trees and all asphalted.

Graham informed me that the average width is double that of the streets and avenues of Berlin or Paris and, though I have never visited Germany, I can confirm that Pennsylvania Avenue appeared to me to be even finer than the Champs-Elysées though my attention was somewhat distracted by Bertie who had plunged his hands inside my blouse and was playing with my hard little titties at the time.

This brings me neatly to the freedom of intercourse (of the social kind!) in Washington. We checked into the grand Hotel Buckingham and deposited our luggage there. The two boys shared a large double room, while for the sake of propriety Molly and I were allocated our own single apartments, though I knew full well that we would rarely have the chance to sleep in our own beds – not that either of us particularly wanted to! Anyhow, Molly pleaded the need to rest as she was suffering from a slight headache, so we left her in the hotel while the boys took me with them to see Senator Easthouse.

As I have intimated, it is in Washington, more than anywhere else perhaps, that the effect of democratic institutions on the habits and customs of the American people are most conspicuously seen. If Jack is not as good as his master in Washington, no such equality prevails anywhere else in the whole, wide world.

Senators, deputies, and ministers of state are common objects here. During sessions of Congress, all the great leaders gather together and the hotels, public offices, the walks of the capital are almost alive with the notabilities of the nation. I rubbed shoulders with many of them and it must be said that there was not the least affectation of superiority on the part of any of these gentlemen. So free and affable were their manners that they invited, rather than repelled, intrusion.

Bertie and Graham escorted me to the offices of Senator Jonathan Easthouse, a senior senator whose main interest was environmental affairs. In true Washington fashion, we walked into his chambers unannounced.

'No-one seems to be around,' commented Graham. 'Let's see if the Senator is in his private office.'

And without so much as a by-your-leave we ignored the 'Private' sign on the frosted door and trooped into the Senator's office. We should have knocked, as I told the boys somewhat severely, but we didn't and so were treated to the sight of the good-looking tall young senator, his trousers and drawers down by his ankles, having his stiff cock lustily sucked by a stark naked auburn haired young girl who saw us enter, but who was determined not to lose contact with that rigid shaft she was working in and out of her mouth.

'Don't let us interrupt you,' said Bertie.

'Damn right I won't' drawled Senator Easthouse. 'Come on now, Cecilia, suck out my spunk!'

The girl's blood was on fire and she took the thick cock in her hands, frigging the shaft as hard as she could, whilst just titillating the ruby head with her tongue, licking all round the mushroom dome as his prick swelled and stiffened to outrageous proportions. He heaved gently so as to work it in and out of her mouth and then, with a tremendous 'Oh!' he spurted his seed down her throat in great gulps of white froth which she swallowed with evident pleasure.

'Ah, that's better,' said the genial senator, extracting his now turgid cock from Cecilia's mouth and hitching up his drawers and trousers. 'Now perhaps I had better explain just what Cecilia and I were doing.'

'I don't think that's necessary,' said Bertie. 'It was quite obvious what you were doing!'

'No, no, no. It would be wrong for you to get the wrong end of the stick.'

'Well, Cecilia got the right end of the stick!'

'Ha, ha. Yes, well, never mind about that. The fact of the matter is that I have been reading this important new book on making love by some Belgian doctor . . .'

'Not David Lezaine, by any chance?' said Graham.

'Yes, that's the man.'

'Well, what an extraordinary coincidence. Doctor Lezaine is a friend of Jenny Everleigh here. You recall, perhaps, that you asked us to present Miss Everleigh to you when we telegraphed that we were visiting Washington?'

'Of course, of course. So pleased to meet you, Miss Everleigh, though I must admit to a certain embarrassment by our first encounter, seeing me being pleasured by this adorable wench.'

'Not at all, Senator, I've seen quite a few cocks in my time and yours is certainly in fine fettle. But what a small world it is, for we met Doctor Lezaine on the train this morning and he has invited us to his club this evening for dinner.'

75

'Heavens alive, how strange. Well, it is thanks to your good doctor that you found me as you did. For in Chapter Four of his new book he lays great stress on the need for complete spontaneity and variety in sexual relations. So as I spontaneously felt the need to have my penis sucked and as Cecilia is always more than willing to oblige . . .'

'Fair enough,' grinned Bertie. 'We will blame the dirty doctor! However, Jonathan, you have not introduced us to this beautiful lady.'

'Oh forgive me,' said the Senator. 'Mr Graham and Mr Bertie Sand, Miss Jenny Everleigh from England, may I introduce my personal assistant, Miss Cecilia Goodbody, a well-named girl if I ever I saw one!'

Still quite nude yet possessing the most assured *sang froid*, the lovely Cecilia shook hands with us. Oh, she was a beauty, of some twenty-five summers, rather above the medium height, light auburn hair, slightly gold in tint, deep blue eyes, set off by dark eyebrows and long lashes, a full mouth, richly pouting cherry lips and a brilliant set of pearly teeth. Her luscious charms greatly appealed to Bertie and Graham whose trouser fronts stuck out openly as their cocks rose to attention as they viewed her magnificent swelling breasts, round and firm and topped with large red nipples. The whiteness of her belly was set off below by a bushy mound, covered with light curly red hair through which I could just perceive the outline of her slit.

She stood blushing very slightly as Bertie and Graham gawped at her lovely body. My blood was up as well and I had a fancy to gamahuche her there and then. She must have known of our feelings as smiling slightly she said: 'There is nothing unnatural about feasting your eyes and firing your imagination, gentlemen. My goodness, are those revolvers in your trousers or are you just glad to see me?'

And then with a self-satisfied smile parting those luscious lips, she patted the smooth marble skin of her belly and then playfully parted the lips of her cunt and she began to frig herself gently, moving a couple of fingers in a restless kind of fashion backwards and forwards between the vermilion lips of love.

'Do English girls have juicy cunts, Miss Everleigh?' enquired the cheeky minx.

'I have never had cause for complaint,' I replied as the delicious girl took my hand and made me sit beside her on a long leather couch.

'I would like to find out for myself rather than simply take your word for it,' she murmured, slipping her hand under my dress till it rested on the silky covering of golden hair that covered my own delicate notch.

'May I play with your pussey?' she inquired.

'Most certainly, if that is what you wish.'

As if in a dream, I undressed until I too was naked. Her soft lips rested gently at first and then with increased urgency on my own. I opened my mouth beneath their persuasive pressure and the next thing of which I was conscious was a warm friction that journeyed knowingly from the base of my throat to the valley between my breasts.

Cecilia moved her head downwards as I whimpered and her probing mouth and fingers played on my body with a sure and sensitive touch. She pulled my long legs apart and nuzzled her rich lips around my curly blonde bush, playing with my cunney and sniffing its sweet odour. 'M'mmm, you have a lovely little pussey, darling. My, how warm and inviting it is inside! How it sucks and envelops my fingers. If only I had a prick I would fuck you so beautifully.'

She separated my legs as far as possible and my own hands clasped her rounded bum cheeks as her tongue flashed around my dampening pubic mound. I looked down and saw her pretty hair bobbing up and down between my thighs as I arched my body upwards to meet the thrusts of her darting tongue. She slipped her tongue through the pink lips as she licked between the inner grooves of my clitty in long, thrusting strokes. My cunney was now gushing love juice and each time Cecilia tongued me my clitty stiffened, even more eager and pulsating, wanting more and more

77

until I exploded into a marvellous all-embracing spend. She lapped up the juices wallowing in their sweet taste as I moaned out my delight.

As soon as she sensed that I had spent, Cecilia lay back and now it was her turn to lie on her back with her legs apart and her hands busy rubbing her hairy cunney provocatively.

I rolled myself on top of her and our breasts crushed together and our pussies rubbed furiously against each other. I slipped a finger into her now soaking cunt and rubbing harder and harder until her little clitty turned as hard as a little stiff cock. I slipped a second and third finger through to her juicy cunt and spread the lips out wide as she gurgled with pleasure. My head was drawn irresistably down and soon I was sucking away with all my might. Her body was jerking up and down which added to the excitement as I worked my tongue until my jaw ached, teasing over the soft, curly pussey hair.

Her juices flowed like honey as I moved my hands up to clutch at her swollen nipples, rolling them against the palms of my hands. How Cecilia wriggled and twisted as my tongue revelled in the thick creamy emissions. Our emotions quite carried us away, my tongue whipping wildly over her clitty until she was gushing so much that the juices were streaming down over my face. Gasping and trembling, she motioned for me to stop before she collapsed.

Of course, this sensual drama had greatly affected the three men. The tall, broad Senator was first to shuck off his clothes and he raised his eyebrows questioningly, asking me if I would let him fuck me. I was agreeable so I nodded my acceptance and with one bound, his arms were around me. We lay together on the couch and his tongue moved downwards from my mouth, circling first one nipple, then the other, teasing, tasting until they hardened. His mouth closed upon one whilst his fingers pinched the other, kneading, sucking as I purred with pleasure.

Almost immediately he lifted his head and his mouth

claimed mine, his hard tongue thrusting as his fingers slipped suddenly between my thighs, sliding across my bush, pressing harder, parting the petals of my cunney lips. Then his body was on top of me and I felt his hard cock following the path his hands had blazed. He gripped my hips and pushed forward and I felt his prick slip between the lips of my wet pussey, easing it in gently but I really felt full up and satisfied as his mouth nuzzled against my breasts and he sucked the pink, tight little rosebuds until they were as hard as his cock that was now ramming in and out of my cunney. I gasped with pleasure as I felt him penetrate me up to the hilt and as he built up his rhythm, I could feel his balls swinging heavily against my bum cheeks.

Soon I could feel the waves rippling through my body. 'That's it!' I shouted. 'Nice and quick now. Now push harder; push, push, aaah!' Closing my eyes and moving my head from side to side, I could not control my cries as I thrust my hips upwards to meet the thrusts of his strokes, driving him deeper and harder inside me. Then we both spent almost together. First I came and not only were all my limbs moving in violent convulsions, but my strong cunney muscles were contracting, squeezing and milking his huge thick cock. I wrapped my legs around his strong body to pin him against me with his thick shaft still jammed inside my cunt.

Almost instantly, I felt his hands squeeze my titties as his prick throbbed wildly and shot hot copious injections of spunk gushing into my cunt. Never before and indeed never since then have I fucked with a man who ejaculated so much jism as Jonathan Easthouse. We hugged and kissed as we sat up to see that Cecilia had now recovered and that she had assisted Graham to pull down his trousers and pants and was happily playing with his naked prick that stood up proudly as she rubbed up the shaft to its massive full erection.

For a while she toyed with his great cock and balls, caressing them in her gentle hands, kissing them lightly until suddenly she sucked him into her mouth and began to masage his shaft with her lips and tongue, holding the thick base of his prick in her hands. Then she eased her lips back, running her talented tongue over the head before her lips closed over the knob and she sucked in at least three inches of his thick shaft into her mouth.

He could not fight against the quick climax that was building up inside his balls. With a hoarse cry, Graham shot deep into her throat, gagging the pretty Cecilia who could not cope with that huge prick as she pulled his cock from her mouth so that the last spasms shot the hot spunk over her cheeks and chin. She smiled as she rubbed her face in his crisp pubic hair then ran her tongue around the tip of his cock, capturing the last drops of semen that had oozed out as his prick diminished to half limber. She sucked hard on it to draw out any more spunk that might have remained there.

Poor Bertie was now the lone non-participant, but soon his natural reserve had broken down and he dropped his trousers, taking out his cock. I thoughtfully padded over to help pull the swollen shaft free. I began giving him a steady tossing and I could see the rich red head straining to keep in his love juice as I pulled the shaft between my breasts. This enabled him to tit-fuck me, splashing jets of jism over my nipples as his shaft quivered between my fingers.

We would have fucked for longer and of course the boys were all for prolonging our stay for that very purpose but the good Senator was determined that I should see more of his fair city and meet some famous people. As I have intimated, access to public men in America is exceedingly easy. So we dressed ourselves and sauntered out into the fine sunshine.

Senator Easthouse proudly pointed out that the Parking Commission which he had helped to establish had done its work so well that upwards of seventy thousand trees had been planted in Washington. The result of the Parking Commission's operations is that one hundred and thirty miles of shaded walks are provided for the use and enjoyment of the citizens of the capital city.

Many of the public buildings are quite splendid and, seeing a particularly fine mansion of slightly greater pretentions than the rest, I inquired of Senator Easthouse the name of it.

'That building, Jenny, is the White House. Would you like to step inside and have a look around? It is all open to the public. Come on, if the President is in, I'll introduce you to him,' he said lightly, as if such an event would be very easy to arrange.

We walked in and I was surprised to note that there were no horse guards at the gates, no sentries at the doors, no policemen in the lobbies nor any such officials anywhere. There were some clerks at their desks in some of the rooms who appeared to be engaged in writing or transcribing public documents and who pursued their labours apparently without noticing the visitors who passed and repassed them, pausing only when they were applied to for information.

While I was looking around, a portly gentleman of the press came up and gave a cheery greeting to Senator Easthouse. 'How do, Senator, I'm Hal Freedman of the *New York Herald*. What brings you here? Are you going to have a meeting with the President?'

No disrespect was intended (or taken) by the familiar mode of speech. The democratic institutions of the United States are probably responsible for this extraordinary familiarity with which citizens speak to one another. Personally, I find it most refreshing. I remember seeing a Member of Parliament push his way through a crowd at the Changing of the Guard, saying quite pompously: 'Make way, make way for a representative of the people' and, bless me, the people did leave a path for him. There would be no tugging of forelocks over here – more like tugging of foreskins and a shout of 'Go and fuck yourself!' or hopefully a more droll response. According to cynics, familiarity breeds contempt. It is not so in America for here, on the contrary, it is more the outward show and semblance of personal regard.

Anyhow, the Senator replied that this was a simple private visit to show the White House to 'a pretty young lady from England.'

'Well, in that case,' drawled Mr Freedman, pointing at one of the more elderly clerks, 'have a quick word with old Moore over in the corner desk. He is gathering names of people who wish to meet the President who will be here very shortly.'

'Can I really meet the President?' I asked in astonishment.

'Of course you can, my dear,' said the Senator. 'He always sets aside part of the morning to meet visitors so I'll just pop over to Mr Moore and put you on the list. Graham, Bertie, come with me and I'll add your names too.'

Mr Moore agreed without hesitation to add our names to his list and the boys and I were shown into an apartment which Mr Moore explained was kept for the purpose. The Senator, who had met the President many times, took the opportunity to take a short stroll with Mr Freedman and exchange the latest gossip around town. No restriction at all was placed in the way of anybody who wished to obtain audience. Everybody was free to come and everybody was welcome who did come.

When the President entered the room, Mr Moore stood by him to make the introductions, mentioning of course the information about the visitor that had been vouchsafed to him. When my turn came, Mr Moore said: 'Mr President, I have the pleasure of introducing Miss Jenny Everleigh from London, England.'

President Arthur shook my hand firmly and said: 'Ah, Miss Everleigh, I know a little about you from a visitor with whom I have just been enjoying a cup of coffee – the famous medical gentleman, Doctor David Lezaine.'

'Doctor Lezaine has been here already sir? Why, we journeyed here on the same train from New York.'

'Yes, so the good Doctor informed me. I understand you are the grand-daughter of Lady Heather Shackleton? My, I have not seen your grandmother in twenty years but a fine lady. I trust she is well. Do give her my personal and fondest regards.'

'She is well, sir, and will be most pleased to hear that you enquired after her. I did not realise that Doctor Lezaine was acquainted with my family antecedants.'

'He is a very knowledgeable gentleman and seems to know everybody both in the Old World and the New,' laughed the President. 'It has been a pleasure to meet you, Miss Everleigh and I trust I will have the pleasure of making your acquaintance at some future time.'

The rest of the introductions were at times a little more formal and I withdrew with a very pleasant recollection of the affable manners of the first citizen of the Republic.

When we left the White House, a messenger boy came up and gave me a note from Senator Easthouse saying that he had to attend to some urgent business but he and Cecilia would be at the Beesknees Club tonight and looked forward to seeing us there. Bertie said he was feeling tired and would see us back at the hotel, so I was left with Graham to escort me further round Washington.

We stopped at a little cafe just off the Pennsylvania Avenue to rest and enjoy a glass of iced tea. I asked Graham, rather boldly I must admit, who had fucked more girls, his cousin Bertie or himself.

'It is said that all men lie about their sexual prowess, Jenny,' he grinned.

'Oh, I do hope that you are not offended by my question,' I said.

'Oh, no, not in the slightest,' said the handsome young buck. 'I was a somewhat late starter, being sixteen years of age before I crossed the Rubicon. You see, Jenny, I was brought up in the South West in a tiny town called Dixon. There were no more than twenty or so kids of school age and we had to ride four miles over to Durie to attend the little school there.

'It was a really strictly run school and old Doc Hollins

would whip any kid who stepped out of line. There weren't many girls and those who did attend were very closely chaperoned. Well, boys will be boys and all of us were just dying for the moment when we could actually do what we had been practising for some time.'

'Practising?' I asked rather foolishly.

'Taking ourselves in hand, so to speak!' laughed Graham. 'Well, it was a Saturday, just two days after my sixteenth birthday, when my father came to me and told me to ride to Medhurst, the nearest town of any size which was some nineteen miles to the West. Medhurst was a cattle town and there were almost always cowboys in town, ready to make whoopee after those long days and nights in the saddle. It could get quite lively there, I assure you, and there were many bars and houses of ill-repute ready to part the cowboys from their dough.

'I was surprised that Father asked me to ride to Medhurst as usually my friends and I were discouraged at all times from going there, our parents believing that it could be dangerous with all those drunken cowboys and their guns (though there was rarely any shooting, truth to tell). And of course the whole town was considered "low" by the good folks of Dixon and Durie.

'I really could not guess as to why it was so important for me to take the envelope my father gave me to Medhurst and I suspected nothing, even though the address was Madame Rosa's Bear Flag Saloon, which even I should have guessed was a house of pleasure. Perhaps it was because my father was a well respected lawyer and a pillar of local society that I had no idea that this envelope contained the extra birthday present he had offhandedly mentioned when I proudly told him that I had come first in the class in the summer Mathematics and English examinations.

'I rode my horse, Silver, at a leisurely pace – by God, how I would have galloped if I had known what awaited me at the Bear Flag Saloon! I carefully tied him up and walked over to give Madame Rosa the envelope. It was now just about mid-day and the doors were closed, which I thought odd for any saloon. But Madame had been forewarned of my arrival and I had just about time to knock once on the shutters when she opened the door for me.

'I politely handed the letter in and asked if there was a reply for me to take back. "Oh, yes, there certainly is. Look, this letter says that after you have finished here you must go to Solly Rubenstein the tailor to be measured up for a new suit of clothes. Your pa says that you will be all dusty from your ride so before you go, you must have a bath. It so happens that I have just run a nice hot bath for myself but I am in no hurry and will write the reply for you to take back. So please go upstairs, the bathroom is first on the left, and do what your father wants."

'I thought it an odd command, but perhaps my father knew that I had not taken my morning bath as usual that day and had added a hasty postscript to his letter to Madame Rosa. So obediently, I went upstairs and went into the bathroom. I was a little concerned when I found out that there was no key to the lock but I assumed that Madame Rosa would tell any other visitor that the room was engaged. I stripped off and enjoyed the warm refreshment of the water. But before I could take hold of the soap I noticed there was a strange magazine on the stool beside the bath. I picked it up and read the title, *La Vie Secrete de Mademoiselle Babette*. A French magazine, I thought. I'll skim through the pages to see if I can understand much of the text.

Well I nearly dropped it in the bath when I opened it out. For on the first page there was a photograph of a lovely girl wearing only a skimpy bathing suit with one strap hanging over the shoulder and one breast almost exposed to the camera. I turned another page and this time the cheeky girl had taken off both straps and for the first time I saw a pair of naked breasts. My cock automatically began to stiffen and, when I turned to the next page, she had taken off the costume completely and, with her back to the camera, was sticking out her pert little arse. My hand went down to stroke my hardening prick which was springing into life. When I turned the next page and saw this pretty girl posed face on quite nude, I began to rub my prick in a frenzy of lust.

'Then out of the blue the door opened and in walked a beautiful girl who looked the veritable image of the girl whose picture I was tossing over. "Ah, Graham," she cooed. "I see you are enjoying the magazine for which I posed last year. Yes, the magazine is French but the pictures were taken in New York which I visited last spring. They call me Babette in the journal, but my name is really Barbara. My friends all call me Babs. Would you like to be my friend, Graham?" As you can well imagine I was stunned and I let go my cock which quickly began to droop. Babs chuckled as she smooth-ed her hands over the light pink cotton robe she was wearing.

"Come, Graham," she smiled. "Come out of the bath and I will dry you myself with this nice big bath towel." I hesitated for a moment but, as in a trance, I obeyed, hardly believing that this was not all a dream. I shook off the excess moisture as Babs wrapped me up in the luxuriant folds of her towel and proceeded to dry me, taking especial care it seemed of my cock and balls. I was still so nervous that when she removed the towel my prick was still hanging limply. "Oh, my, we can't have you standing at ease," she murmured, taking my cock into her warm soft hand. "Let's make this little soldier stand to attention."

'The spell was broken and I came out of my trance. My penis began to swell as she gently rubbed the shaft with one hand and squeezed my balls-sack with the other. "Is that nice?" Babs asked somewhat unnecessarily, as my tool was now as stiff as a poker. I nodded my head as I was far too excited to reply with any coherence. "Well, if you like that, let us see how you take to this," she added, as she tugged at the sash round her waist that held the robe closed. The sash fell to the ground and she stepped out of it in all her naked glory, her flesh creamy beige, her breasts commanding my eyes, their nipples being so rosy and pointed.

'She smiled again and then she dropped to her knees and to my amazement took my hot throbbing cock and began to lick at the purple headed knob. I almost swooned with pleasure as she proceeded to suck up an inch or two of my shaft. It was all too much and I felt my balls filling with jism. By instinct rather that through knowledge, I plunged my cock hard into her mouth. Babs must have sensed my urgency as she sucked enthusiastically so that I exploded into her mouth, my penis jerking madly as she swallowed my juice. But she could not contend with the copious emission of this first true sexual encounter and my jets of spunk gushed down onto her chin and between her small but jutting breasts.

'After milking my cock dry, she wiped the jism from her chin and titties and sucked her fingers clean. My cock remained large though not quite at its biggest as Babs gave it another rub, working the foreskin up and over my swelling knob. "Goodness, you, have the thickest cock I have ever known for a lad of just sixteen," she said. "And how you spunked! I can normally swallow it all but I felt I was drowning in it with you. Goodness me, look at that lovely prick. It's as hard as a rock again. Yes, you are ready to experience for the very first time the delights of a juicy wet cunt."

'Babs spread the towel out on the floor and lay down upon it. She motioned me to kneel between her legs as she reached out to stoke my shaft very gently for she was concerned that I might spurt my spunk before I tasted the delights of her juicy quim. She guided my yearning cock between her cunney lips and there I let it rest for a moment. I moved as slowly as I could, wanting this glorious magical experience to last forever. What a marvellous joy coursed through my body as I fucked the lovely girl with all the vigour of a young colt.

'I knew that if I moved too quickly I would spend too soon, but Babs enjoyed having a thick prick in her sopping cunt and began groaning with desire, her whole body tickling, licking, rubbing, slithering until I burned with lust as I thrust powerfully in and out of this delightful cunney. "Yes, yes, yes!" she screamed out and, seconds later, I exploded into her, my orgasm as powerful as a rocket sending great globs of hot sperm shooting into her love channel. I could see from the blissful expression on her face that she too was riding the wind with me.

'First love can be idyllic – or disastrous, Jenny,' he concluded. 'I was naive, shy and slightly bewildered by what happened to me, but I was fortunate in having a father who understood my burning need to fuck and who provided a willing partner – albeit for money – for I later discovered that the envelope contained a money order for fifty per cent more than the usual fee charged by Madame Rosa's girls to ensure that my girl would be clean and helpful.

'So I was fortunate enough to make my first journey down the highway of love with a sophisticated lady who understood my needs and catered to my every desire,' added Graham.

This tale had stirred my imagination so I said: 'Graham, I thoroughly enjoyed hearing about your first fuck. I want you to take me back to the hotel now and let's see if your next fuck will be as good as your first!'

It was only a short walk back to the hotel and as soon as we entered I hoisted up my skirt to take off my suspenders. Graham must have also been fired by the recounting of his erotic memories because before I knew it his hands had beaten mine and my suspenders were unhooked and my drawers were being pulled down.

We tumbled onto the bed, tearing at each other's clothes in a frenzy. I reached down and stroked his ragingly hard erection and feverishly I undid his fly buttons and clasped my hand round his thick shaft. I delicately fingered the bulbous knob and found that it was already juiced up at the end. So I bent over and lapped up his sweet juices. Graham was one of the many American men who knew how to suck pussey, a trait sadly lacking in Englishmen, as I believe I have mentioned before, although Molly has since told me that the Welsh appear to have a penchant for it.

Be that as it may, I lowered my cunt over his handsome face, parting my labia with my hands so he could gain immediate access to the moist flesh inside. He began sucking noisily, taking one flap at a time into his mouth and pulling at it, and then he began licking me so that my cunney was now quite slippery. By now, I was bent over, working on his grand, hard cock, running my teeth gently against the ribbed nodules of his prick. Then I sucked in his ruby mushroomed knob and flicked my tongue over the dome, washing it teasingly, working over his ultra-sensitive knob, while my hands fondled his balls. I moved his hands down to my cunney and he slipped in a couple of fingers and he frigged me so beautifully that I felt a strong spend coming on.

'I must have your cock inside me!' I cried out passionately, grasping his shaft as I jammed myself down on his fingers, spreading my legs wide. But there is nothing to beat a hot, thick cock so I leaped off his fingers and moved my pussey down over his twitching thick tool, sitting on him with my bare bum towards him. He grasped my buttocks with both hands and began squeezing them rhythmically as I pushed up and down, contracting my powerful vaginal muscles with every movement so as to feel every millimetre of his lovely big cock. I reached between his legs and took his balls in one hand and started to massage them, running my fingers back along his hairy arse and forward again to his balls, scraping the sack with my fingernails so they writhed in my hand. I was now breathing deeply and he was groaning with ecstasy as I rode him harder and harder, while the bed bumped in rhythm on the floor.

He began to jerk up and down so fast under this stimulation that I no longer had to move but just let him bounce me up and down on his glorious cock, letting the tide of an approaching orgasm take me over. I felt his powerful prick contract and twitch. Together we joined in a mutual spend as with a crash, he sent a torrent of creamy, warm spunk right up inside me. There was so much jism that my cunney overflowed and ran down his cock and over his balls, whilst I lay quivering and totally spent.

We lay there for a while, panting with exhaustion. When we had recovered Graham went to his room for a bath and to change for luncheon whilst I too enjoyed the luxury of a warm tub and a change of apparel. Molly and Bertie had left a note to tell us that they were lunching at the very expensive, but highly fashionable, new restaurant run by Mrs Bickler on East 15th Street, and were then going on to the baseball game at Deacons Hill Park, not far from the famous Arlington cemetery.

'I would prefer a light luncheon,' I remarked.

'So would I,' said Graham. 'A pussey sandwich and a cold glass of beer would be ample fare. But I will settle for some sandwiches and iced tea. If that is to your satisfaction, I will order sandwiches and we can sit outside on the verandah.'

'That sounds lovely,' I said. 'But what is this baseball game all about? I do not know how it is played and I should enjoy going to the match, for I enjoy most sports.'

'Yes, I know you do, Jenny. Indoor sports especially!'

'Oh, do not tease me, Graham. Will you take me to the game?'

'Of course I will, my pet. We have plenty of time to first enjoy our lunch over which I will attempt to explain the rules of the game to you.'

I took notes of his explanation and I enjoyed the game so much more than cricket, though I shall not admit as much when I return home, for my boyfriend, Johnny Oaklands, is a fanatical follower of our native summer sport. Let me attempt to briefly sketch out the rules of baseball.

On the field a square is marked out with sides of ninety feet and it must be so set as to be used diamond-wise. The bases are at the compass points with the batsman, say at south and the bowler (or pitcher as they are called) at north. The north, east and west bases are marked by firmly fixed, square, stuffed bags, and the southern base is made of solid iron sunk in the ground. The ball is slightly lighter than a cricket ball and is covered in white horsehide. The bat is like a Brobdignagian constable's staff, forty two inches in length and two and a half inches thick. Two squares are marked on either side of the southern base for left or right handed batsmen. The pitcher stands in a small oblong called a 'box' fifty feet away and the catcher, the equivalent to our wicket keeper, stands well behind looking for catches. He is well-gloved and wears a kind of inflated blacksmith's apron to protect his body and dons a mask to go up close to catch or take the ball, and throw it to a fieldsman.

Summing up, the game goes like this: a pitcher sends a ball to the batsman who must take (and hit if he can) any one of three balls which the umpire considers fair, when he calls 'strike'; if the batter fails thrice then he is out. A fair ball is one that would or does pass over the plate which forms the home base at a height between the knee and shoulder. Having struck the ball the batsman runs as many bases as he can but risks being caught out by a fieldsman, ball in hand, putting his foot on the base, or touching him, ball in hand, between bases.

The match was between two university teams and the dexterity with which the young players handled the long clubs, the cleverness with which the opposing sides tried to circumvent each other and, above all, the enthusiasm exhibited by the partisans of the competitors imparted an immense amount of spirit and animation to the scene. When one side or the other scored, an organized party of friends among the spectators rose to their feet under the direction of a fugleman and gave a musical cheer of approbation and encouragement. It was noticeable, too, that the girls who were present wore the colours of their teams, just as British ladies at the Boat Race wear the light and dark blue favours of our two great universities.

We met Molly and Bertie during an interval and my dear cousin also announced how much she enjoyed this American sport, 'but it is not so much fun as fucking!' she added, somewhat unnecessarily.

We walked back to the Hotel Buckingham. I may have neglected to mention, diary, that Washington is laid out in the fashion of a wheel with the Capitol for the centre and broad avenues for the spokes. And besides the usual numerical arrangements of streets, there is alphabetical arrangement also. So the thoroughfares on one side of a main avenue are called First Street, Second Street, Third Street, etc, whilst those on the other are known as A Street, B Street, C Street and so on. The system may make for dull addresses but in a land of immigrants, where many do not have the benefit of English as their native tongue, one can understand the need for a simple no-nonsense city map.

On our way we passed the massive National Hotel, by far the biggest in Washington. We took tea there and, as is usual in Washington, the waiters were all negroes who created a most favourable impression by reason of their pleasant appearance, their ready attention to the guests and their orderly mode of discharging their duties. Some of the younger waiters were quite good-looking and Molly must have noticed that I was looking at one handsome young buck because she leaned over and whispered: 'Are you thinking what I'm thinking?'

'I don't know,' I answered truthfully. 'It depends what is going through your mind.'

'I was just wondering whether it is true what they say about black men.'

'What is it said about them, Molly? I do not know what you are talking about?'

'They are supposed to have huge cocks!' she said dramatically.

'What's that about huge cocks?' Bertie enquired.

'Don't worry, Bertie, we weren't talking about you,' laughed Molly to his discomfiture. 'I was just telling Jenny that negroes are commonly supposed to have mighty big pricks.'

'You will see for yourself at the Beesknees,' said Bertie, recovering his good humour. 'You know, Jenny, they put on some marvellous performances based upon the happenings that I understand take place regularly at the Jim-Jam, the famous club in London. I don't know whether you have ever been there?' (Readers of the previous book in this series will recall Jenny's experiences at the Jim-Jam Club in Soho – Editor.)

'I have visited the Jim-Jam and I know all about the Victor Pudendum contests,' I said carefully.

'Ah, well, we have an equivalent competition known as the World Superfuck series but tonight you will be entertained by an erotic cabaret,' Graham chipped in. 'And I'm pretty sure that there will be one or two black performers, including the famous Texas Longhorn.'

Molly and I said we would look forward to this entertainment. We stayed a while in the hotel and I marvelled again at the lively buzz one feels in the big American hotels. They are places of rendezvous for everybody, whether they are guests or not. If you want to know anything, to see anybody, or to go anywhere, you can obtain all the information you require at a hotel. The numerous clerks are always civil and obliging and if they can't, as they say, fix the thing for you, they can usually put you on the track of it.

Should you have an appointment with a friend, he names a hotel in a convenient neighbourhood where you can meet him. The commodious entrance halls are always full of guests, loungers and men of business. People go in and out, look around, take a seat, buy a newspaper or smoke a cigar with as much ease and freedom as our own people go in and out of a public market.

When I commented upon this to Molly she agreed, saying that a fortnight ago, she had occasion to wait for a friend one evening at the Fifth Avenue Hotel in New York. While waiting for her friend, she had the opportunity to observe the incessant influx of visitors to that famous establishment. There were four swing doors of plate-glass to the main entrance. Such was the constant traffic through these doors that seldom was one allowed to settle in its normal position before it was again thrust open. The American hotel is, in fact, as much a public institution as the post office or railway station.

The plan of the evening was to partake of a light supper and then afterwards to go to the Willard House Hotel – the most elegant and exclusive hotel in Washington, where, of course, Doctor David Lezaine was staying. We would meet him there and join him in the audience for the concert of chamber music to be given by a most talented local group of musicians. And then it would be on to the Beesknees.

First, Graham and Bertie decided to shave. I should note here that in the mode of dealing with the hair and beard, the American is distinguished from the Briton. When the hot season commences, many male citizens of the Republic have their hair cut so close that they almost look as if their heads had been shaved! In the same way that persons in England who wore beards or moustaches before our veterans returned from the Crimean war were taken for foreigners, so persons who do not shave in America are generally understood to be strangers or immigrants.

The present fashion is to shave closely, leaving only a moustache if required. Shaving, indeed, is so commonly practised that it has become one of the fine arts. I went with the boys to McGinty's which is the most fashionable establishment of its kind in the city. Long rows of reclining chairs are placed in front of an equally extensive mirror. Here the customers deposit themselves in the easiest of postures while the barber performs his work with all the grace and dexterity of a master at the business.

I chose an elegant black dress with a somewhat low cleavage to wear for the evening's entertainment. The weather was so warm that I decided not to bother with any underclothes except a tiny pair of cotton knickers. I walked along to Molly's room and she greeted me with a kiss and said: 'I'm really looking forward to some fun and games tonight, Jenny. Do you know, I've not bothered with any underclothes except a pair of knickers.'

'Great minds think alike,' I laughed. 'I have decided to do exactly the same thing.'

'Well, if we don't get fucked tonight, we'll never get fucked at all,' Molly declared. 'I hate all the business of undressing. When my blood is up I just want to get on with the job.'

'Oh, yes, but I dislike being fucked with my clothes on. To fully enjoy making love it is always far better to be naked.'

'Yes, I prefer being nude when I fuck. Mind, the boys tell me that it is most pleasurable to see the swell of a pert breasted girl under the covering of a blouse or dress, and then thrill to the sight of her nakedness as she undoes her blouse and a view is given for the first time of her nakedness, the large aureoles tipped by the ruby red nipples that jump up so magically to the touch.'

'I can understand that,' I replied. 'Is it not equally true of us that little can equal the joy of first stroking the bulge between a boy's legs whilst kissing and then undoing his flies and bringing out his naked cock in all its glory, the erect shaft throbbing in your hands as you gently rub it up and down to its maximum length?'

'And then suck the luscious sweetmeat until it squirts jets of jism in your mouth!' Molly cried out. 'Ah, Jenny, do not get me too fired up or I shall have to frig myself off before we have begun!'

I gave my pretty cousin a glass of water to cool her down for it would be a shame to start our fun too soon. In any case, we had promised to meet the boys at seven o'clock promptly and it was now five minutes to that hour and I have always been a stickler for punctuality. So Molly composed herself and as we made our way downstairs, she told me that she was glad that Senator Easthouse was coming to the Beesknees as he was reputed to be a superb lover. 'He does not possess an enormous cock,' said Molly confidentially. 'But I do hear that he has great staying power, and that's an ability younger men sometimes lack. Not that I'm criticizing either Bertie or Graham,' she added hastily.

We walked down to the hotel's lounge where Graham and Bertie were already waiting for us. They looked very handsome and smart in evening dress.

After supper we walked the short distance to Willard House and we met David Lezaine who – surprise, surprise – was escorting not one but two pretty girls! There was just time for introductions to be made before we had to take our seats for the concert.

'How nice to see you again, Jenny,' beamed Doctor Lezaine. 'Let me perform some introductions. Mr Graham and Mr Bertie Sand, Miss Jenny Everleigh, Miss Molly Farquhar, may I introduce my two charming hostesses for this evening, Miss Victoria Wollie and Miss Ellie Doodle.'

As ever, the good doctor had picked the most choice companions. Victoria was an extremely attractive girl of some eighteen years of age. She was slightly shorter than average with a cheeky little face set under a mop of bright auburn curls, and her slim, athletic frame was set off quite delightfully by a close-fitting dark green costume in the modern style. Ellie was also a most exquisitely pretty girl, with gold-dusted blonde hair, not dissimilar to mine, and sensually large, blue eyes. She was dressed in what I am sure was a Paris creation; a low-cut gown which set off her blonde colouring to great effect. I am sure I saw Bertie's cock wriggling against his trousers as he shook hands with the two girls and exchanged pleasantries.

The concert was held in a most elegant ballroom and indeed there must have been an audience of at least two hundred people for the concert by the gifted amateurs of the East Washington String Quartet. My eye was taken by the good-looking young first violinist and for the second time that evening Molly, who was sitting next to me, read my mind. 'Are you looking at that gorgeous violinist?' she whispered. 'He could fit his bow to my cranny whenever he liked!'

I was pleased to find out that neither Victoria (who insisted we addressed her as Vicky) nor Ellie were girls who stood upon ceremony in the European fashion. 'Did I hear you mention the violinist?' murmured Ellie softly. 'The young man with the long, dark hair and those dark, fiery eyes – is that who you were talking of?'

'That's right,' said Molly. 'Does he play as well as he looks?'

'Even better – with or without his violin,' Vicky chipped in, which caused us to burst out into a fit of the giggles. 'Not that I have ever seen his instrument, worse luck!'

'What's his name?' I asked Vicky and our new friend informed us that the musician was one Bernardo Rubeno, a Mexican from south of the border. He was discovered by, of all people, an English traveller, Sir Philip Lintern, the well-known musicologist whose taste for *recherché* erotica had taken him to Mexico City. Sir Philip brought the young man to Washington and he had now made his home here. Through the munificence of the textile magnate Lewis Segal, Bernardo was able to study under Sir Philip's famous friend, Professor Breslau, the great music teacher, who set up a new academy in America after being forced to flee his native Russia because of the persecutions of the Jews in their Pale of Settlement.

David Lezaine leaned across and said: 'I can hear what you girls are talking about – be quiet now and if you keep that way through the concert, I'll ask Bernardo to join our party at the Beesknees.'

Being quiet while the musicians played was hardly a chore for any of us. Bernardo and his friends played quite beautifully and one of the pieces in the programme was an all-time favourite of mine, the Beethoven Quartet No. 6 in B flat. The first movement is light and happy and although the richly melodious Adagio is of a serious and reticent nature that Beethoven requested to be played *si deve trattare colla piu gran delicatezza* (with the greatest delicacy), the music draws to an almost wantonly carefree *prestissimo* conclusion. We applauded vigorously and as an encore Bernardo gave us Schubert's Minuet with Two Trios, lovely little pieces often thought of as *Deutschetanze*, dance music probably written by the sixteen-year-old Schubert for family parties.

Afterwards, David Lezaine was as good as his word and, although Graham and Bertie were none too pleased, Bernardo, who spoke perfect if slightly accented English, accepted the invitation to join our party with alacrity. I told Graham and Bertie not to be jealous for after all, neither Molly nor I had complained when two pretty nubile young girls were added to the group.

But the boys still looked a little out of sorts as we climbed into the carriage that would take us to the Beesknees. 'I am sure you have a bigger cock than Bernardo,' Molly assured Graham, as she stroked his prick tenderly. 'And yours is probably thicker, Bertie. You are both, I am sure, far more considerate and better lovers so do cheer up.'

Her wise words had the desired effect and we were all in good spirits when we arrived at the imposing mansion that housed the Beesknees, the most exclusive private club in Washington, membership of which was carefully restricted to a chosen few.

Downstairs, the club consisted of one large common area in which all members could come and go as they pleased with an adjacent small dining room. Upstairs, however, there were twelve private salons, which each member could book and be assured of total privacy and discretion. Only two hundred members could belong to the club at any one time and the waiting list was at least three times that number. Last year, only three members resigned but the strict rule was first come, first served. It was, I hasten to add, an all-male bastion, although women were freely admitted as guests, on the understanding that any member signing in a female as his guest would donate ten dollars to the funds of the Beesknees charity, the American Society for Literacy, which provided free tuition in the writing and reading of English for immigrants, a most worthy objective in a country where the population come from so many different parts of the globe.

Our party sat in the luxuriously furnished general area and David Lezaine ordered French champagne for us. There is a perfectly acceptable American champagne grown from French vines transplanted to California, but despite the terrible expense – I am sure the Moet cost twenty-five dollars a bottle – David insisted that we enjoy the real article.

'When will Senator Easthouse and Cecilia arrive?' I inquired.

'Oh, they will be here later,' replied David. 'President Arthur's private secretary, the formidable Mrs Conn sent round a personal note for the Senator because the President wanted his opinion on some matter or other and he could hardly refuse.'

'Well, I see no reason to postpone our fun because there will be late starters,' piped up Ellie, who I was soon to find possessed the tastes of a tribade, but who was also not averse to the male sex. 'David, I understand that you have booked a room upstairs?'

Molly, whose tastes encompassed a variety of pleasures, nodded her head in agreement as she stroked Ellie's thigh suggestively. 'I would very much like to join you, Ellie,' she said.

'And so would I!' said Bernardo quickly.

'In good time,' said the little minx. 'Yes, Molly, you, Jenny and Vicky come upstairs with me and we'll prepare ourselves for the boys. After all, someone has to wait here for the Senator. Don't worry, though, gentlemen, we'll get in the mood and be ready for you, say, in three quarters of an hour's time.'

Bernardo, Graham and Bertie looked depressed at this announcement, but the wise head of the older man, David Lezaine, knew what was in Ellie's mind and he said: 'That's perfectly all right, Ellie. We'll finish this fine champagne and join you later. Here, my dear, take this key. We have number twelve for the evening. Off you go.'

So we four girls trooped upstairs to Room Twelve on the second floor and what a magnificent suite it turned out to be. The main room contained a magnificent four-poster bed and, when I sat on the bed, I noticed that the top had a large mirror stretched across it, something I had never seen before.

Vicky saw my surprise and said: 'Have you never seen a mirror there before?' I confessed that I had not and the delightful girl explained that for many people, including herself, it was a great stimulation to be able to see one's partner from a fresh angle, so to speak, whilst engaged in *l'arte de faire l'amour*. 'Let Ellie and Molly show you,' she said, motioning me to sit on the comfortable chaise longue by the window. The rich velvet drapes were closed but the electric lights gave off a pleasing though not glaring luminescence.

Meanwhile, Molly and Ellie were already sitting on the bed cuddling and kissing in the most lascivious manner. Ellie expertly unbuttoned Molly's dress and as their mouths glued together in a most passionate kiss, she moved Molly's shoulder straps down and pulled out my cousin's bare breasts, so firm yet so soft to the touch. Ellie's lips brushed Molly's titties, then licking her lips, the lovely girl opened her mouth wide and her pink tongue swirled round and round the aureole, licking and nibbling the nipple up to a firmness as her hands went underneath Molly's dress. To her delight, she discovered that Molly was naked underneath her dress and, throwing up Molly's skirt, exposed her pretty cunt, daintily fringed with blonde hair, to general view.

The two girls quickly divested themselves of the remainder of their clothes. Now absolutely nude, Molly lay back on the bed with Ellie, whose equally attractive pussey was lightly covered with blonde hair, now thoroughly aroused; as Molly moaned with pleasure, Ellie began to kiss Molly's breasts, licking all round in circles then jamming her lips on the proud, stiff nipples. Ellie then slipped her hands under Molly's legs and grasping her bum cheeks, pulled the girl towards her so she could nuzzle her head between Molly's legs. Vicky and I watched entranced as we saw and heard Ellie's clever tongue slurp in and out of the juicy little slit while Molly's body jerked up and down with excitement.

I was thoroughly enjoying the exhibition and I hardly noticed Vicky's hand move under my dress and inch its way upwards. Almost automatically I opened my knees slightly, allowing her hand to sink between my thighs, then closed them again, trapping her long fingers against my warm crotch. Then the pretty girl boldly kissed me full on the lips and said: 'Come now, Jenny, why should those two have all the fun?'

Why indeed, I asked myself so I let myself lie back on the chaise longue, spreading my thighs wider to make it easier for Vicky whose fingers began to move, tracing the shape of my pussey. As her fingers began to explore the outline of my labia, I breathed in, letting the sweet warmth of her touch flow through me and I sighed as her fingertips parted the dampness of my lips and I gasped as she teased the hooded nub of my clitty. Now my breathing became ragged as I pressed her hand into my pussey, impaling myself on her stabbing fingers. My own hands too were now busy, roving over Vicky's luscious breasts, teasing up the taut nipples to a fine erectness.

We undressed in a trice and joined Molly and Ellie on the bed. Those two blonde tribades were now engaged in a mutual gamahuche with Molly sitting astride Ellie with her dimpled little bum raised up as she leaned forward to bury her head in Ellie's silky blonde bush. Ellie was meanwhile holding Molly's bum cheeks, spreading them to give full access to her juicy crack which Ellie rubbed against her generous mouth. Now Ellie fastened her mouth to Molly's slit and slipped her tongue in and out of her sopping muff out of which Vicky and I could clearly see Molly's superb three-inch clitty projecting from the pouting lips.

Vicky and I each had our hands over each other's cunts and were rubbing them against our glossy bushes. I was particularly taken with Vicky's thick auburn moss. She was like a sleek pampered kitten as she arched her back with delight as I explored further between her legs and I tingled all over as the warm, welcoming lips of her pussey opened magically under my gentle probes. I now slipped my hand between her firm bum cheeks and began to frig her wrinkled little bottom-hole which made her wriggle a little uncomfortably. I switched back to her pussey which she obviously preferred as she began cooing like a dove as I transferred my hand to her cunney, rubbing my knuckles against her crack until she was breathless with excitement.

Then, still frigging her pussey, I began to kiss her aroused titties, licking and sucking them until they were as hard as little bullets. I kissed her flat tummy and downwards, ever downwards to the firm curve of her pubis, slithering my lips gradually until they were directly over her quim. I could taste her salty juices and I sucked hard on her throbbing little clitty, prodding it to little series of pleasure peaks. I frigged her passionately, burying my mouth in the moist, succulent padding of auburn curls, until the lovely girl screamed: 'Oh! Oh! Jenny! You make me spend, my darling!' and her love juice came flooding out of her cunney all over my mouth and chin.

Well, this was all very well but I had not yet spent and what I really needed was a proud young prick in my pussey! Luckily, dear Molly could always read my mind for as this thought flashed through my brain, my sweet cousin (who had already finished off Ellie to their mutual satisfaction) brought out a delicately fashioned black rubber covered dildo from under the bed. It was the same shape and size as an average cock and, oh, how lovely it felt as Molly, with a happy smile, firmly placed the rounded bulb between my legs, letting it nest momentarily in my wet bush.

She nudged it gently between my receptive cunney lips and as she increased the pace and depth of insertion, my pussey began to produce love juices copiously as her clever manipulation of this wonderful imitation penis brought me off time and time again. I squirmed with excitement as I spent beautifully. We then formed a daisy chain, with Molly parting Vicky's cunny lips with her dildo as Ellie slipped her hand under Molly's plump bum cheeks from behind and played with her pussey while I lay face downwards across Ellie, whose mouth flicking across the wet grooves of my cunt set off a lovely tingling glow throughout my body. My own hands were free to fondle and caress the tempting curves of Vicky's exquisitely proportioned breasts, and I rubbed her tawny titties up to new peaks of hardness against my palms as the delicious girl swirled around in ecstasy from the double stimulation of my fingers tweaking her nipples and Molly slipping her dildo in and out of her pulsating pussey.

We all seemed to spend together which was quite delightful. As I have said before now, few men can suck pussies as well as girls but I still maintain that nothing can beat the feel of a stiff, thick cock in one's cunney. And when Ellie asked me if I had enjoyed our little whoresome foursome, as she put it, I politely said that yes, of course, it had been most pleasant, but that I still preferred cock as my main course.

'I have no wish to appear ungrateful,' I continued. 'But I feel as if I have eaten a particularly tasty *hors d'oeuvres* and now I am ready for the entrée.'

'You won't be disappointed,' drawled Ellie. 'I agree that a good-sized cock on a boy who knows how to use it takes a lot of beating, but I do so love being licked out and it appears that only girls can bring me off. Like just now, Molly used her tongue so cleverly to lick and lap gently from my bum to my clit. I was already quivering with anticipation when she parted my bush and began moistening my cunney lips. And oh, the wonderful way she sucked my juices, flicking her tongue all round the grooves of my cunney.'

'Yes, that's all quite splendid, but don't you enjoy sucking a cock?' I asked.

'Most certainly,' replied the pretty girl. 'I do find a most delicious sensation thrills through my frame whilst I am sucking a cock. I particularly enjoy running my tongue over the knob which all boys enjoy immensely.'

'Do you swallow the spunk, Ellie?' asked Molly curiously

'Goodness me, what a question! Of course I do. The very sensation of the jets of hot sperm spurting into my mouth brings on an instant spend.'

'That's funny, because although I also enjoy licking and sucking my boyfriend's prick, I just cannot bring myself to swallow his jism,' said Vicky. 'It upset my last beau because when I felt him coming I stopped sucking his cock and finished him off by rubbing his shaft.

'I also enjoy doing that because I can then see the spunk shoot out of his cock which you can only feel if his shaft stays in your mouth. If I mistime the boy's spend, I discreetly use a handkerchief to spit the spunk into as soon as possible.'

'We must each try to pleasure our partners,' said Molly firmly. 'But this must be a two-way process. Your old boyfriend had no right to be annoyed because you wouldn't swallow his jism. One must always respect the wishes of your lover. Too often men think of us as mere receptacles in bed and, indeed, out of bed, only fit to wait on them hand and foot. Mark my words, the time will come when women will revolt against the idea of being chained to the bedroom and the kitchen and against the second-class way of life allotted to us by a male-dominated society.'

Ellie, who was a most intelligent girl, was very interested in what Molly had to say. 'Are you one of these "wild women" we hear so much about in our newspapers?' she queried.

This question was all Molly needed to hear and I sighed, for female emancipation was Molly's pet hobbyhorse and I knew that a brief lecture would follow. Actually, I was feeling a little tired and I was happy to close my eyes and listen to my dear cousin spout forth, especially as I agreed with almost everything she had to say.

'I'm no wild woman,' said Molly, clearing her throat. 'But I want to wake up all members of our sex to the waste continually going on in the lives of countless thousands of our sisters whose lives are blighted or wasted by a long course of mental and physical deterioration. Women must take full part in the government of all nations and must free themselves from the tyranny of the bearing and rearing of vast families, together with the incessant work of running a home often in straitened circumstances.

'The domestic treadmill must be modified and women be allowed equal opportunities as men to progress in the world. Of course, there will always be women who prefer to be housewives and good luck to them. But there are many of us who want to taste other experiences.

'My friend, Sir Charles Dilke, has written: "Men are going forward so fast that the rift between the sexes will become wider if women are to continue living on the old lines and never take a step in advance." And Charlie is quite right. We must go forward for our own sake and for the sake of generations to come.'

'You are quite the politician,' said Vicky admiringly. 'You must speak to Senator Easthouse about your ideas.'

'I mean to,' said Molly. 'But I'll be sure to suck his prick first!'

We burst our laughing and Ellie opened a bottle of champagne, one of a number that lay in a huge ice-bucket on one of the ornamental tables, and served us all with a glass of that most refreshing drink. I do so love champagne and I was glad to hear David Lezaine tell a gathering that an occasional glass was most beneficial to good health – I am sure he is right.

While sipping my champagne, I noticed that the pictures on the walls were of the distinctly rude variety. One depicted a beautiful dark haired naked girl seated on the lap of her handsome lover. Between her voluptuous thighs her cunt is seen delightfully gorged with his standing cock. Her arms are round his neck and her pretty face is turned up, beaming with the satisfaction she is experiencing in her well-filled pussey. Another picture was in fact a photograph of two nude couples presenting their pricks and their cunts in the most exciting view. One boy was shown pressing the soft bum cheeks of his lovely partner who was holding his standing prick in a loving grasp, whilst the other chap was squeezing the ample breasts of his beloved, who was bending over with her tongue round the dome of his cock, her hands cupping his pendulous balls.

We continued to consume champagne for the next ten minutes, when there was a timid tap on the door. 'Come in,' shouted Molly. The door slowly opened and there was the handsome Bernardo, the violinist whose bow we all fancied to fondle.

'Come in, come in!' we chorused. Bernardo obeyed the command shyly, closing the door softly behind him. His eyes fairly goggled when he realised that here in this room he was the only man with no less than four lovely girls, three blondes and a redhead, all quite nude and all obviously more than ready for a good fuck. He was lost for words as we calmly decided who should be first to enjoy making love with this good-looking young Mexican musician.

'I think it only fair that we toss for it!' said Ellie and that unwitting *double entendre* set us all laughing our heads off.

'I know, I know,' squealed Vicky. 'Let's all guess how big his cock is and the girl who guesses nearest gets the first fuck.'

'What a splendid idea,' I said. 'But have we got a tape measure?'

'Yes, it so happens I have one in my bag,' said Vicky, scrambling across the bed and bending over the side, reaching down for her purse. The sight of her luscious nude buttocks and inviting arse crack caused Bernardo to tug at his crotch where a bulge began to appear.

'I want to fuck,' he said hoarsely.

'In a moment,' I said firmly. 'If you are a good boy you can have us all, providing you have the stamina.'

'I can fuck all night,' he boasted.

Now, in my experience, it is the big mouths who make the worst lovers, though naturally this does not affect the size of their cocks. To repeat myself *ad nauseam*, it is not the size that counts but what the owner of the equipment does that pleases a girl. However, to return to my narrative, we all gave our estimates as to the length of Bernardo's tool.

'Five and three quarter inches,' I hazarded, being the first to try my luck.

'Six and a quarter inches,' said Ellie.

'I'll go for six and three quarters,' said Molly. 'Any advance on that?'

'I'll try seven and a quarter inches,' said Vicky. 'Though as I never win anything in lucky dips, I am sure that Bernardo's penis will probably be one of those stubby thick pricks which have strength but no length.'

Bernardo understood enough English to understand what was being decided and he gave a big smile and said: '*Por favor*, do not I get to guess the length of my own prick?'

'Why, don't you know how long it is?' said Ellie with some surprise.

'I don't need to measure to know that I am fortunate to possess a fantastic pussey pleaser,' he announced, unbuttoning his shirt. 'But more important I know how to use it as many ladies will be pleased to testify.'

'Well, let's see how you measure up,' said Vicky, who knelt down beside Bernardo who, tantalizingly, had turned his back as he pulled down his trousers. With a flourish he turned around and four pairs of feminine eyes swerved to his crotch. I have to confess, diary, that Bernardo had not boasted idly. His semi-limp cock was shortish, but thickly barrel-shaped, with the broadest dome I had ever seen. Vicky was well pleased by what she saw and reached out and took his shaft in her hands. Her warm touch was all Bernardo needed and his prick began to stretch, stiffening and swelling perceptibly, his foreskin peeling back to reveal all of that huge mushroomed knob. When his prick stood at full erection proudly against his flat belly, Vicky took hold of the tape measure and, placing one end against the base of the shaft, carefully calculated the length of the throbbing length that twitched against her fingers.

'So who has won our little cock contest?' I asked.

Vicky grinned in triumph. 'See for yourselves, ladies. Bernardo, your prick measures fractionally over seven inches so I declare myself to be the winner.'

Ellie, Molly and myself were too genteel to query Vicky's judgement so we obligingly made room on the bed, Molly and Ellie sitting on one side and me on the other, giving Vicky the room to enjoy her fuck in comfort.

She wasted little time, first gently stroking Bernardo's thick cock and then after giving the purply dome a quick kiss, she took hold of the shaft and guided the boy down onto the bed. He lay down on his back with his magnificent truncheon standing stiffly upwards as Vicky climbed on top of him and, turning her bottom to his belly, lowered herself onto his cock, opening her legs and straddling over his trunk, giving us an enjoyable view of her bushy mound with its covering of curly silken red hair.

She sat still for a moment, enjoying the sensation of repletion and possession so delightful to each participant of a loving fuck, before commencing those soul-stirring movements which gradually work our heated desires to that state of frenzied madness which can only be allayed by the divinely beneficent ecstasy of spending.

Bernardo pulled himself upwards so that whilst Vicky bounced happily up and down on his cock he could grope her sopping cunney. 'Oh, heavens, Bernardo! Bernardo! Bernardo! Do, do come, darling while I am spending!' screamed Vicky as she reached her own peak of passion. 'Yes, Yes! There, ah, I feel it, how deliciously hot! Oh, Bernardo, that's marvellous!' She groaned with excitement as his flood of boiling seed inundated her sopping pussey which had so tightly enclosed him. It was a very quick fuck but none the less extremely satisfying, for they both wanted a short but sweet coition.

The sight of the lovely couple fired us three spectators and Molly, Ellie and I clambered up onto the bed to take part in a mutual canoodling session. Without the slightest shame or reservation, we engaged in the most passionate kisses, our tongues probing and sliding into each other's mouths.

Ellie concentrated on Bernardo, whose long, sinewy cock fast regained its former stiffness under the ministrations of her wet, generous mouth. Meanwhile, Molly had climbed on top of the lucky lad and pulling open her cunney lips with her fingers, began to rub her open pussey across his handsome face. Bernardo took hold of her firm bum cheeks and in a trice his tongue was darting in and out of her juicy pussey. I was left with Vicky, whose legs I was fondling, stroking the silkiness of the naked warm flesh of her thighs. I moved my hand upwards to caress the sticky wetness of her soft cunt.

'Darling, ohhhh, darling . . . Jenny . . . that feels so good . . . please, darling, finish me off!' she murmured in my ear, licking the lobe, an action that always drives me to lustful desires.

I allowed my loving fingers to slide into her eager, waiting cunt. Sensing the sex juices welling within her, my finger slipped in and out in unhurried rhythm as her body rocked backwards and forwards in time with my gentle probings. Now I pulled her legs apart and nuzzled my lips around her red pubic bush as her pussey opened wide to receive my darting tongue. I placed my lips over her erect little clitty and sucked it into my mouth, where the tip of my tongue began to explore it from all directions and I could feel it growing larger as she twitched up and down with excitement. I twirled my tongue round and round that sensitive little button. She began to moan loudly and I could taste the sweet juices flowing out of her. Oh, her pussey was so delicious to taste and I was determined to suck her even harder. Pushing my mouth hard up against her, I moved my entire head back and forth until the lovely girl was dripping wet and quivering all over.

She was now quite desperate for release so I moved my tongue even quicker than before along the succulent grooves of her cunt, licking and lapping the juices that ran down like a stream, mixing with my own saliva. With each stroke, Vicky arched her body in ecstasy, pressing her now fully erect clitty up against my flickering tongue.

'Aaaaah! Aaaaah!' she squealed and then let out a little yelp of delight as she exploded in my mouth, her clitty jerking violently against my tongue as she spent profusely.

I looked up and saw that Ellie had coaxed up Bernardo's prick into a fine state of stiffness and she was tonguing the pulsating knob with warm, caressing strokes as Molly jiggled happily over Bernardo's face as he lapped away at her dripping notch. I decided to join in the party and slipped a hand underneath Bernardo's heavy balls whilst adding my tongue, which was still wet from Vicky's spendings, to Ellie's. She nibbled away at his knob, biting and tickling it with the end of her tongue as I stroked the underside of his shaft with my fingers, capping and uncapping his helmet until Ellie drew his knob fully between her lips, drawing hard as though she wanted to suck down to the very bone. I transferred my hands back underneath, gently manipulating his ponderous balls through the soft wrinkled skin of his hairy bag. I could see that Bernardo was close to spurting for his prick began twitching uncontrollably and his moment of truth was obviously but moments away.

Ellie jammed her mouth down, sucking and slurping noisily as he pumped spurt after spurt of hot, sticky cream into her mouth. She lifted her head at each lavish spasm, gobbling and gulping every last drop of juice out of that pulsating prick until it began to shrink back from its ramrod hardness and the dome slipped back underneath the foreskin.

Molly had climaxed beautifully over Bernardo's mouth

but this left me still unsatisfied, which seemed a most unfair state of play. However, with all the exciting happenings going on, I had not seen David Lezaine enter the room and slip off his clothes. He was now standing by the bed and Vicky was on her knees lustily sucking his swollen cock.

'My dear Vicky,' said the good doctor. 'I would far rather fuck you than simply spend in your mouth. Take your luscious lips away from my prick. Yes, yes, that's right, my sweet, that's just perfect. Don't worry, I'm not about to spend! Now bend over with your legs apart and lay your hands down on the bed in front of you.'

She willingly obeyed and David was given the lovely sight of her firm young bum cheeks, two beautifully rounded globes in between which lay the puckered little wrinkled arsehole which winked up at him as he parted the cheeks of her gorgeous bottom. He edged his velvety looking gleaming cock towards it but Vicky turned her head and cried: 'Oh, David, don't bugger me tonight. I would far rather you would fuck my cunt, if you don't mind.'

'Your wish is my command, cherie,' said David gallantly and he pulled her long legs further apart until he had fair view of the pouting pink lips of her juicy cunt. She reached out behind her and grasped his prick, guiding it between the willing lips of her insatiable cunney.

Effecting a safe lodgement for the head, he buried the shaft to the hilt with one forceful thrust and his heavy balls flopped against her bouncing buttocks. He thrust again and again as he clasped her to him, his arms round her tummy and with one hand dipping in and out of her sopping muff as he swiftly brought her to a tingling climax.

'Dayvid, Daaayvid!' she screamed happily. 'Ah, push harder you darling man. Fuck me hard, now, slam that great cock in and out of my cunt!'

He withdrew almost all of his red and swollen shaft and then thrust forward hard again and again, pumping his cock in and out as she bucked and jerked wildly until, with a convulsive final shudder he poured luscious jets of cream into her in an ecstasy of enjoyment and they sank down on the bed together into the bliss which follows the opening of the gates of love's reservoirs.

But we were still short of cocks, so I was delighted to see the door open to admit Graham and Bertie who, fresh to the fray, undressed in record time and plunged into action.

I was slightly put out when Graham made straight for the auburn-bushed pussey of pretty Vicky but Bertie grabbed hold of me and we kissed and cuddled and I pulled my hand up and down his twitching shaft.

'Can we wait just a little before we fuck?' I asked Bertie. 'I should first very much like to see how Vicky handles Graham's extraordinarily big cock.'

'Yes, that should be worth watching, especially as David Lezaine tells me that she has a deliciously small notch,' he replied.

As we watched, Graham kissed her breasts and belly and then he pressed his lips downwards as if drawn magnetically to that red-haired bushy mound. I craned my head over to look at his tongue licking at her clitty and the girl arched her back upwards as the big man prised open her pussey lips with his fingers, sinking them slowly into her slit which was already dribbling with juice. He then moved up between her legs and rubbed the head of that monster prick up and down her crack until the lovely lass pleaded with him to put it inside her yearning cunney.

Teasingly, he inserted just a little piece of the red-plumed helmet which her pussey lips gratefully enclosed. Molly, ever the upholder of women's rights, tut-tutted and grasped Graham's huge cock, pulled it out and pulling his foreskin right back, pushed three inches of prick back into Vicky's cunt as she squealed with delight. Molly moved her head down to suck his balls as Graham and Vicky built up a slow rhythm.

Bernardo and David Lezaine were now both aroused and they were relieved by Ellie who sat between them with a cock in each hand and her long fingers, working as though

112

they possessed a will of their own, frigged their cocks deliciously. Indeed, Ellie was so expert in this sensual rubbing that both men were brought quickly to the inevitable result and they spent copiously, the froth shooting out of their pricks over her hands and sprinkling her blonde mossy mound and belly with spunk.

Molly now left Graham and Vicky to fuck together and she slipped her left hand cunningly between Ellie's firm buttocks and began to frig her puckered little bum-hole, while her head moved down to nestle in that glossy bush of blonde silk as she kissed and tongued the mount of love in a frenzy of delight. Molly's tongue revelled in slipping in and out of Ellie's soaking bush out of which a superb little clitty was already projecting from between the pouting lips. The girl wriggled with pleasure at this tribadic stimulation.

As she tongued happily away, Molly's own bum was high in the air and Bernardo jumped behind her and passing his hand round her narrow waist, handled her bush quite freely and slid two fingers into her longing quim. Her bum cheeks wriggled joyously as Bernardo wet the head of his cock with spittle and drove his rigid prick into Molly's arsehole, deeper and deeper as she rolled around, still keeping her head firmly between Ellie's legs, nibbling away at the swollen clitty as Ellie rubbed herself off against Molly's generous mouth. Molly was lucky enough to possess an extremely tight bum-hole for Bernardo's cock rode in and out of the tight sheath of her bottom, pumping and sucking like the thrust of an engine. Molly reached back and spread her cheeks even further and the movements of her rump became more hurried as Bernardo shot jets of spunk deep inside her bottom.

It was time now for Bertie and I to begin our loving fuck which began with the tenderest of caresses with Bertie kissing, licking my nipples and rolling them carefully between his teeth. I took hold of his shaft which gleamed white in fine contrast to the purple knob and so I rolled him on his back and began to tease it with my tongue, pulling back the foreskin and licking the swelling knob, savouring its tangy taste. My mouth was as wet as my cunney as we turned ourselves into a glorious *soixante neuf*, my mouth on his stiff prick and his eagerly devouring my pussey. His tongue slid up and down my labia, easing them apart and circling my tingling clitty.

This was so exciting that I knew he could not be far from a climax. I felt his ball bag tighten and his back arched up from the bed, thrusting his slippery wet cock deeper in my mouth. I helped him by cupping his bum cheeks in my hands and I slipped my lips as far down the shaft as I could possibly go without gagging, feeling his wiry pubic hair tickling my nose. His spunk came crashing into my willing mouth as I pulled him harder into me, milking his tool of every drop of warm, white froth.

But Bertie's cock was now *hors de combat* as he rolled off me but ever the gentleman, David Lezaine moved over to take his place, his stiff cock probing the entrance to my loveslit and remained there until I eased open my thighs to admit the swollen head. 'I want it all!' I gasped and he obeyed, pushing in his shaft inch by inch. I succeeded in taking his full erection inside me and he stayed still inside me for a moment. Then he moved slowly in and out and I was getting even more excited watching his prick appearing and disappearing inside my cunney. Then he began to quicken the tempo and closing my eyes and rocking my head from side to side, I matched his rhythm. Soon I could feel the waves rippling through me and as David released the jism from his balls, my cunt accepted his spunk and sprayed my own juices on his cock as we mutually enjoyed the currents of erotic energy that passed through our bodies.

We opened some more champagne for we needed to refresh ourselves for a final chain fucking session with Bernardo fucking Ellie, Molly working her dildo in Bernardo's bottom whilst her own bum was being fucked by Bertie. Vicky was lapping at Molly's cunt whilst her own pussey was being fucked by Graham who was sucking my titties as I leaned forward to be fucked from behind by David as I nibbled and chewed on Vicky's rosy nipples.

We changed positions to try out further combinations and the gentlemen manfully gave satisfaction to each and every one of us until we could no longer coax their pricks up to further work. In fact, I had enjoyed the fucking immensely but enough was enough and over-indulgence in even this, the finest of all sports, only leads to an uncomfortable soreness the next day.

So we washed and dressed ourselves and spent the rest of the evening downstairs in conversation with other members of the club. I must note here of my appreciation of the Beesknees rule which forbids smoking and chewing tobacco in one section of the main rooms. I especially dislike the common habit of chewing tobacco. It hardly exists in New York but in Washington, where men from the old Slave States and the wilder regions of the Far West are to be found, this unpleasant habit is common. Even in Congress itself it was painful to notice how often individuals discharged their tobacco with little regard to the rich carpets that covered the floors. Spittoons are in general use in America. Some are made of leather and are as big as footstools. Others are made of metal, as ornamental as flower vases and as large as coal boxes.

All the hotels are supplied with great numbers of these utensils. They are dotted over the floor of the halls, disposed in rows along the corridors, placed in corners on staircases and no bedroom is considered furnished without at least one of them.

It was almost two o'clock the next morning before we left the Beesknees for our hotel. As you can imagine we were all speedily in the arms of Morpheus and we enjoyed a late breakfast at about ten, after which the boys and Molly went for a stroll while I, dear diary, confided these intimate secrets to your care.

We plan to take the express train back to New York later this afternoon. After a few days, Molly and I will be on our travels again, but this time on our own, northwards to view the famous Niagara Falls. This is a journey I am very keen indeed to undertake as I could hardly take a holiday in America and omit this amazing natural wonder from my itinerary. It is a shame that Bertie and Graham are otherwise engaged, but I am sure that we shall not want for any masculine company, if such is desired.

August 17th, 1884

We enjoyed a most enjoyable railway journey back to New York. The inevitable newsboy harangued us but departed happily enough after Bertie bought a variety of Washington papers to while away the journey.

I must record how I was struck by the spirit of flippancy that seems to characterize all American newspapers. Trivial and serious subjects are treated in the same manner and a great fraud or a grave crime is discussed with as much seriousness as a social scandal. The ordinary run of newspaper writers appear to be afflicted with an irrepressible desire to imitate the humorous style of Mark Twain or Josh Billings.

And while it is a well understood doctrine in Britain that newspapers are bound in honour to abstain from opinion concerning the guilt or innocence of an accused person until he had been tried, no such reticence appears to be observed here. Offenders are tried in the newspapers long before they come into court at all. During the legal proceedings in great cases, comments are freely made on the prospects of the prosecution, the demeanour of the prisoner or the conduct of the judges concerned in the case. If contempt of court is a recognized offence in America, it is certainly a law that is continually flouted without any apparent prospect of punishment.

Nor is the law of libel more frequently put into force. If it were, there is scarcely a journal that would not have at least two or three suits on its hands every week! But when I commented upon the fact that public men were denounced in the press as fiercely as if they were cut-throats, Graham said: 'Oh, nobody here pays any real attention to the newspapers.'

One interesting feature of American newspapers is the personal advice column for readers. I mentioned this to David Lezaine who answered: 'These advice columns can be very useful for people who do not have the resources to find out valuable information for themselves or who are embarrassed to ask intimate questions.

'I receive many letters from patients and their friends and I am sure that if the questions and answers (everything published under the strictest rules of confidence and anonymity, of course) were made available to the wide audience of a city newspaper, such a feature would be most instructive as well as entertaining.'

Bertie looked up from his paper and said: 'I think that a newspaper medical advice column is a very sound idea. It reminds me that I was going to speak to you, David, on behalf of my young cousin Edmund who is worried about the size of his testicles. He is only seventeen but he tells me that his balls appear to be much smaller than those of his friends and he is concerned about it. Can you reassure him, Doctor, that he has nothing about which to be fearful?'

'Of course I can,' laughed the good doctor. 'For a start, Bertie, there is absolutely no medical connection whatsoever between the size of the testes and their function, which is, of course, to produce sperm. Testes average a length of about one and a half inches and a width and thickness of around one inch. Also, and you might have noted this, the left testicle usually hangs lower than the right. As in the case of pricks, size is absolutely immaterial, but if your cousin is still worried after you have conveyed my reassurance, he should consult his own doctor who will soon put his mind at rest.'

'I would like to ask you a question,' said Molly brightly. 'I have a friend who is very self-conscious about the fact that the outer lips of her pussey are larger than most other girls. Does she have anything to worry about?'

'No, no, no, not at all,' said David firmly. 'Vaginal structural variations are commonplace and, contrary to popular belief, have little to do with any sexual orientation. Neither your friend nor Bertie's cousin should waste further time or emotional energy about minor differences in physical makeup.'

'Well, while we are conducting this fascinating brains trust,' said Graham, 'I suppose I should ask you about an old friend of mine who experiences some discomfort when his penis stiffens up to full erection as his foreskin is too tight to slip easily over his knob. Is there anything you can suggest, short of circumcision, the prospect of which would terrify him, as he is only nineteen years old and hopefully has years of fucking in front of him.'

'Oh dear, it is a great shame that his foreskin was not removed at the onset of puberty,' said David, pursing his lips thoughtfully. 'Believe me, the operation is not so dire, although perhaps I would recommend the services of a Jewish surgeon who is experienced in the removal of the foreskin to allay all doubt. But frankly, although your friend would have to undergo an anaesthetic, of course, the procedure is perfectly simple and any competent surgeon could easily perform the operation.

'I assure you that your friend really has very little to worry about. Mind, his rod will be out of action for about three weeks afterwards, but surely this would be a small price to pay to be able to enjoy fucking. However, I would advise him to seek more than one opinion, though I am sure that he will receive the same answer from any reputable medical man.'

In a lighter vein, I asked David whether the old country saying that a big nose was the sign of a large cock possessed any validity.

'It's absolute poppycock, Jenny,' he declared, 'as is any old tale about overall physical appearance having any bearing on the size of a man's prick. It so happens that Graham here is a big man and he has the fortune to possess a cock of immense size, but a tall man of ample frame may well be endowed only with a small cock. As you Americans say, it's simply the luck of the draw.'

We had a few further questions to put to David Lezaine but I cannot recall them all or indeed his wise answers so, dear diary, I shall have to omit them. However, all this talk of *les affaires d'amour* made Molly and I feel rather randy so we slipped off our clothes and stripped David quite naked and laid him out across a seat with his large cock waving stiffly in the air. Molly was the first to attack the purple domed knob by licking it up to bursting point and then she swung herself over his face so that her luscious blonde pussey was directly over his mouth. The good doctor frigged her moist hairy crack with his tongue as I jumped onto his flagpole-like cock and began riding up and down on it to our mutual satisfaction, while Molly and I embraced and fondled each other's breasts, flicking our titties up to little bullets.

After this, we both sucked his cock and balls till he mounted Molly and plunged his prick deep inside her, while I fondled his large balls and worked a finger in his bum-hole to excite him to the very utmost. David was in fine physical shape, for even this did not exhaust him because he gama-huched us in turn before burying his great bursting cock one more time in Molly's bum-hole. She leaned forward to grab Bertie's cock, which was now outside his trousers and standing stiffly to attention, and frig him to emission, while David spurted copious jets of spunk into her bottom.

We had dressed and composed ourselves by the time dinner was to be served (afternoon tea as we know it in Britain is rarely taken, although the beverage itself, of course, is available at any meal in the large hotels).

Then Graham, who as I mentioned some time back was a regular bookworm and a fount of knowledge, said to us: 'You know, I have always been fascinated by the mechanics of sexual arousal. For instance, as Jenny knows full well, the merest touch of her dainty hand on a cock will make that organ swell up and stiffen almost immediately. Similarly, if a man is fortunate enough to be allowed to stroke her naked breast or bushy mound, his cock will straightaway rise to attention.

'Yet there are other little nooks and crannies in a man's body that also stimulate a limp prick. I mean, several men enjoy having their nipples nibbled gently. I quite like having mine squeezed or better still brushed lightly with a nail.'

'I don't like that at all,' chipped in Bertie. 'But I will confess to possessing the most sensitive thighs. I think that even when I reach four score years and ten, if my nurse scratches the back of my thighs, I'm sure that I will be able to manage a cockstand.'

'There are some men who want girls to massage their feet and suck their toes,' intoned David Lezaine. 'Similarly, I know of a patient who was aroused by a girl stroking his ankle. All quite fascinating, gentlemen, and absolutely harmless, of course. Indeed, when I counsel men who are suffering from impotence, I attempt to discover if there are other parts of the body beside the obvious ones that create sexual urges.'

'I do not wish to boast but I would wager that there are few cocks that I couldn't suck up to attention,' said Molly. 'I have found out that if I flick the knob with the edge of my tongue and then roll it around in my mouth, sucking in as much of the shaft as possible, well, it is simply a question of how long the man will hold out.'

Unfortunately, although I would like to have participated in this interesting and highly educational discussion, I found myself being eased into the arms of Morpheus and I slept soundly until we reached Grand Central Station.

After we unpacked our belongings at the Stuyvesant Club, I noticed that a letter addressed to me had been slid under the door. It was an invitation from Count Sasha Labotsky, who owned the famous Russian Tea Rooms patronized by all the top families in Manhattan. He wanted Molly and myself to spend Sunday afternoon as his guests at Barnum's Circus Show which was playing on Coney Island for the weekend. As our journey to the Niagara Falls was easily postponed briefly, after consulting Molly, I wrote back to the Count thanking and accepting his kind invitation.

Count Sasha later telephoned us to ask if we would like to extend the trip to a weekend at his cottage in Long Branch, New Jersey. I still find it difficult to speak freely into a machine but Molly has no such qualms and will happily speak into the telephone for, sometimes, an interminable length of time.

Anyhow, as the weather was now really very hot indeed and Graham and Bertie had matters of business which would entail them being out of town for a few days, we accepted this further hospitality. Molly told me that the Count would make up a foursome with his handsome friend Conrad Clive, the financier and sportsman, and that we should have a jolly time together.

We took the train to Long Branch on Friday morning and I must say that the pleasant trip was made even more agreeable by the equally pleasant company. The Count was a typical Slav, outgoing, extrovert and zestful. I was also most taken with young Conrad. He was twenty-five years of age, (almost twenty years younger than the Count), tall, with a shock of dark hair, gleaming white teeth and a perfect skin, coupled with the confidence that comes from good breeding or wealth, or both.

When we reached the station, a buggy was waiting to take us to Sasha's house. I should explain that Long Branch is a colony of detached cottages, deserted in winter but filled with fashionable occupants during the summer season. Hotels and houses, all provided with verandahs and painted and constructed in a most picturesque fashion, stretch along the sea beach for several miles. During the height of summer, when the heat of the sun is tempered by cool Atlantic breezes, many thousands of the wealthier people may be seen reposing here, surrounded by a profusion of flowers and creepers.

Sasha's cottage was small but well situated just off the beach. When the coachman brought in the luggage, I whispered to Molly about whether there were more than two bedrooms. Before she could answer my query, Sasha said:

'You two girls can share the big bedroom and Conrad and I will bunk together in the smaller room. Unless, of course, anyone can think of any more convenient arrangements.'

'Let's see how we go,' I declared. 'Your plan seems most acceptable to us so if you gentlemen will excuse us, we will unpack and change our clothes.'

'Fine,' said Conrad with a flashing smile. 'Don't put on too many clothes though, Jenny Everleigh. Remember that you must never gild the lily!'

I accepted the compliment by returning his smile and said: 'I'll try not to disappoint you. Now, how about the domestic arrangements? Have you any servants here, Sasha?'

Our genial host roared with laughter and replied: 'A servant? Jenny, my dear, this is America, the New World where Jack is as good as his master.'

'Sasha is right, ladies,' added Conrad. 'We Americans resent the idea of inferiority so much that no-one will accept the designation of servant, except the poor Negroes, who have little chance of advancement because of the prejudice against them, or new immigrants, who do not regard domestic service as servile labour.'

'However, do not despair, my dears,' soothed Sasha. 'We have two local girls who come in to wash the linen and attend to other chores. As to the cooking, it will be my pleasure to prepare your meals. I enjoy cooking, you know, and at my restaurant I am too busy by *les affaires* to cook, though I must say that my chef, Herr Manfred from Vienna, is far more accomplished in the kitchen than I.'

In fact, we were destined never to taste the delicacies that Count Labotsky wished us to try, though as Sasha plans to visit Europe next year, perhaps I shall have an opportunity then to sample his dishes.

For while we were all unpacking, a message arrived for Sasha from his wealthy friend Radleigh Berbeck, the newspaper magnate, who owned a magnificent house just half a mile away. Sasha had told Mr Berbeck that he was bringing some guests down for the weekend and the generous tycoon was insisting that we dine with him that evening.

'If you prefer to stay here, I can refuse the invitation,' said Sasha to us.

'Well, if it is all the same to you, ladies, I would very much welcome the chance to meet Mr Berbeck. My company has a small financial interest in his newspapers and I would be most interested to meet him,' said Conrad.

'We don't mind at all, do we, Molly?' I said, and my sweet cousin nodded her pretty head in agreement. 'But if I may be permitted to make a personal remark, I just must say that in England, a young man like yourself would never be able to build such a large business in so short a space of time.'

'Ah, this is America, the land of opportunity,' said Conrad. 'But I do not claim all the credit for my father left me a sizeable fortune which, thank goodness, I have so far invested wisely.'

'You are altogether too modest, Conrad,' said Sasha. 'After your father's tragic death in that dreadful railway accident at El Paso, you were left with many responsibilities as the eldest son – to your mother, your brothers and sister and to the many people who depended upon Colonel Clive for their livelihoods.

'In just over three years, through your own business acumen, you have trebled the value of your late father's estate, if the *New York Sun*, which, incidentally, is owned by Mr Berbeck, is to be believed. And you are, and you cannot deny the fact, one of the most eligible bachelors in New York City. I just cannot imagine how you have escaped the bonds of matrimony for so long, Conrad, so make the most of your freedom. Remember, I have a wager with your dentist Ronnie Donne, that you will be hooked by the end of the year!'

Conrad blushed and said: 'You must never believe what you read in the *Sun*, Sasha. If there is no news, I declare that the journalists simply make up the news as the day progresses.

'Take no notice of Sasha, ladies, but I fear I can do little to prevent him acting as my unofficial, unpaid and unwanted publicity agent. Enough, now, Sasha, or I won't come into the Tea Rooms ever again!'

'Oh yes you will,' said the Count good-humouredly. 'I know you have your eye on that buxom new waitress who arrived from France two weeks ago. Remember, my French is even better than yours so I could fully understand why it took eight minutes to order Russian tea and a piece of strudel!'

'I am delighted to hear that you are both proficient at French,' said Molly. 'It looks as if we are truly set for a jolly evening!'

Anyway, we dressed ourselves up for the evening and Mr Berbeck sent round a carriage to drive us to Berbeck Lodge, though I should have enjoyed a slow stroll in the cooler fresh evening air. 'Is Mr Berbeck married?' I asked.

'I am glad that you asked the question, Jenny,' answered Sasha. 'Yes, he is married but he and Mrs Berbeck prefer to, ah, live separate lives. I believe his companion tonight will be Sally Thompson, the literary critic of the *New Jersey Enquirer*, another of his newspapers.'

Our host welcomed us most civilly. He was a broad-shouldered man in his early forties, not tall but well-built and with a rugged face which was of a florid complexion. Sally Thompson was perhaps a few years older than Molly and myself. In her mid-twenties, perhaps, and certainly she was a most attractive girl. Her shiny very dark brown hair was worn simply, framing her pretty face and forming a level fringe on her forehead, and her large brown eyes indicated an intelligent and observant mind. We all got on famously from the start and as we went in to dinner I looked up the staircase at the fine gildings and mirrors and had the feeling that we could well find ourselves staying the night in this luxurious house.

As ever in America, all formalities were quickly disposed of and we enjoyed a most delicious meal.

Now, before I record what happened after the liqueurs had been served, dear diary, I must observe for the benefit of any who may read this journal that the kind of uninhibited jollification that took place is fine with me, so long as it flares up spontaneously. I have never been keen on the discreet pre-arranged party between carefully selected couples who are aware, by virtue of being sent a copy of the short invitation list, of what is afoot.

But I must not digress for indeed the writing of these pages is taking far too long out of my marvellous Yankee holiday.

Radleigh had suggested that we take our liqueurs at table, which was a curious request. As none of the gentlemen smoked (perhaps the day will eventually dawn when men realise that the vast majority of girls abhor the smell of tobacco), we sat back and enjoyed the fine selection on hand. Fine French brandy was the choice of all except Sasha and myself. He plumped for a small glass of kummel, a white spirit which he told us was based upon the humble caraway seed and was consequently excellent for the digestion. I tried the kummel and found it most delicious and can recommend it most wholeheartedly. Sasha explained that it was a drink much favoured by wealthier folk in Poland and Russia. I wonder whether it is available back home. [Kummel enjoyed some popularity when it was generally introduced to Britain early in the twentieth century. It is particularly popular in golf clubs where it is sometimes known as 'putting mixture' – Editor]

We were now fully at ease and totally relaxed when Radleigh called for some more coffee. He pulled the service cord behind him and to the greatest surprise of all us guests, the doors opened, and a most divine girl appeared holding a large silver coffeepot. I could hardly believe it, but this was the pretty young maid who had taken our coats when we had arrived at Berbeck Lodge. The pert, well-proportioned young minx was wearing only a white, translucent robe that covered yet revealed, to our astonished gazes, the proud swell of her uptilted firm breasts, the dark circles of her aureoles which surmounted them and the hard richly red titties which pressed against the thin covering. Down below the material wafted out with every barefooted step and we were treated to the sight of the brazen, dark triangle of her bush. She filled our coffee cups and Sasha took the opportunity to stroke one of the magnificent breasts that nudged his shoulder whilst his cup was refilled.

Our talk had been stilled to a low murmur as the girl then put the pot on the table and, instead of retiring, with a feline grace sank to her knees and disappeared under the table. I guessed her purpose when Molly gave a faint gasp and I knew that the maid had pulled down my cousin's drawers from the amazed look on Molly's face. Radleigh affected complete disinterest in what was occurring and said to me: 'So, Jenny, I gather then that you do not find American newspapers respectful?'

'Not very much, but at least they can never be accused of dullness. But I do find some of the material printed here occasionally scurrilous and vulgar,' I replied to his amusement, keeping as I did one eye on Molly and Conrad who were wriggling about most curiously. I drew back my chair and walked round to where they were sitting, or rather moving around in extraordinary fashion in their chairs. I lifted up the tablecloth and saw that the maid had plunged her face up between Molly's thighs and was busy eating her pussey whilst she was attending to Conrad's standing cock, which she had taken out of the confines of his trousers, with her hand.

Molly trembled all over and her violent shuddering was proof that she had climbed the highest pinnacle of pleasure. I peered under the table again and true enough, the maid was now lustily sucking Conrad's thick prick. I looked up and saw that Sally had moved to take my place next to Radleigh and looked smiling and at ease. I guessed (correctly as I later found out) that she had the magnate's prick in her hand as he prettied his fingers about her bushy mound.

Sasha had crept up behind me and had placed one arm round my waist and the other over my shoulder so that his hand was placed over my left breast which he squeezed gently as he nibbled my ear, whispering: 'I think it is time we adjourned into the lounge.'

Conrad was jerking up and down in his chair as he shot jets of frothy cream into the maid's mouth. She gobbled up his juice, smacking her lips and then scrambled to her feet, tearing off her transparent dress so we were treated to her delectable nudity in toto. The lovely girl then took hold of Conrad's cock, which had not shrunk back to flaccidity, and rubbed it up back to a fine state of erection, and seeing the bulge in Sasha's trousers, she unbuttoned his fly to take out his stiff standing tool. Then, holding both men by their cocks, she took them into the adjoining room on which there were four broad divans with brocaded silk cushions strewn discreetly upon them. The rest of us followed as the girl whispered something to the two steeds in whose hands, so to speak, she held the horny reins.

She then let go the two throbbing penises as she lay face down upon a black velvet divan, raising her glorious bum cheeks. Her two charges tore off their clothes. She wriggled a little and the polished orbs of her bottom gleamed, their whiteness accentuating the slightly gingery hue where the cheeks met and rolled in one upon the other to form the deep and secretive cleft. Beneath, she showed clearly the thickly furred bush of her cunney, whose rolled lips evinced a lascivious moisture amid the silky dark curls.

Conrad was now positioned behind her, passing his arms around her to caress her firm young breasts and drawing her close as he took one arm away to smooth the majestic *rondeurs* of her bum. He let his hand linger on her bottom crack and passed his fingers below to feel the soft, wet lips of her pulsating quim. This sight so aroused me that I took hold of Conrad's swollen prick and lasciviously placed it at the entrance of her puckered little rosette. She turned her head and licking her lips, said: 'Go on, sir, you may fuck my bottom with my full consent. I know you gentlemen prefer to spunk inside me but I would be worried at this time of the month to let you finish inside my cunt. And in any case, I like to be bottom-fucked now and then.'

So Conrad joyfully went to work with a will and her bottom responded to every shove as his prick shunted, thrust, emerged and then thrust in again. He sheathed himself fully as he brought her bum into his belly.

Conrad was a considerate lover and as his cock moved in and out he snaked his right hand round her waist and diving into the curly bush, massaged her erect little clitty as he spurted in her with a flood of gushing jism that both warmed and lubricated her back passage. And he continued to work his cock back and forth so that it remained stiff and hard until with a 'pop', he uncorked it from her now well lubricated arsehole.

Emboldened by passion and a wildness of desire, Molly now stripped off her clothes and on her knees began to kiss and fondle the young girl who lay exhausted on the divan, still recovering from the energy-sapping bottom-fuck given her by Conrad. Not for the first time, I noted that my cousin Molly's figure was well nigh perfection, a vision of such wondrous subtle curves that I am sure the three so far unused cocks around me fairly leaped to attention. The perfect snowy orbs or her breasts were tipped by two of the largest brown nipples I have ever seen and her cunney was well furred with blonde hair, the light curls massing in the crispest of triangles about it. Her hips had the fullness of young womanhood, her thighs were plump without merging into fatnesss, whilst the slender curves of her calves and her sweetly rounded knees were themselves a true enchantment.

The two girls rolled off the divan onto the thick carpet and lying on her back with her legs splayed, the maid enjoyed Molly's tongue twirling around her pussey, while Radleigh quickly divested himself of his remaining clothes and kneeling down besides the tribadic twosome, offered his bursting cock to the maid who wetted the knob with her tongue before taking him into her mouth in long, rolling sucks.

Sally too was now in a state of nudity and her body, smooth and white was like a perfect plain of snow which appeared the more dazzling from her thick growth of dark black hair which curled in rich locks inside the hirsute triangle between her legs. Sasha aided Sally in removing her clothes and I must confess that I made no complaint as I found myself forced firmly down onto the carpet with Sally there besides me, kissing my lips and stroking the insides of my thighs.

When her fingers found the lips of my cunney, I heard myself simply sighing with pleasure. After a few moments, instead of just lying passively, I put my arms around her, holding that gorgeously soft body close to me as her fingers continued to rub my dampening cunt. I fondled her high tilted naked breasts, tweaking the nipples between thumb and forefinger as she sank a finger into my now squelching slit. I squirmed with the joy of it all as her thumb prodded against my clitty and her mouth closed around my own engorged nipple, licking and sucking it up to its full erected state. With her clever thumb still attacking my erect little clitty, she began slipping her fingers in and out of my cunt faster and faster. Her fingers were not half the thickness of a good-sized cock, but the way she used her digits was superb.

The thrill between my thighs was spreading now and growing all the time as my body surged to the same rhythm as Sally's fingers. I spread my legs wide and clasped Sally's hand in mind, pushing her fingers even deeper inside me as I waited for the force of my coming orgasm to erupt which it did within seconds, shuddering through me as my sticky love juice came spurting out over Sally's fingers.

Sasha now joined the fray and we rolled him over on his back and together sucked his prick. It was the first time I had shared cock-sucking and it was certainly a most exciting experience, meeting Sally's tongue as we licked Sasha's meaty shaft and let our tongues meet together on top of the uncovered purple dome.

'Would you like the first fuck, Jenny?' she asked politely. I nodded my acceptance of the kind offer and I knelt across Sasha, arching my hips to give him a good view of my pussey. I spread my cunt lips wide with my fingers and frigged myself. I was gratified to see his fleshy prick grow by at least another half-inch and a blob of white juice appeared in the slit of his knob.

Holding my cunney lips open, I eased myself down over Sasha's cock and gave a gasp of satisfaction as it filled me totally. I slid up and down the shaft and Sasha met my thrusts with his own, jamming his cock upwards as I rammed down, squeezing my cunt muscles, knowing that soon I would milk that lovely prick of all its love juice.

Sasha began to groan and I felt his cock throbbing and pumping as I ground down on him one last time, screwing my pussey around him, gripping his cock in a vice as with a hoarse cry and a shudder that racked him from head to toe, he squirted a torrent of hot spunk inside me, filling my entire tunnel until I could feel it splashing inside the rear wall of my womb. I jerked my head backwards and abandoned myself to thrashing around on his still stiff prick. As fortune would have it, I managed to spend a second time just before his cock softened and shrank down to its normal size.

The question now to be considered was whether Sasha could take on Sally who straddled the prostrate man, her curly muff of black pubic hair touching his lips as she bent down to take his soft cock into her mouth. But alas, no amount of her generous licking and sucking could stiffen Sasha's resolve. However, young Conrad came to the rescue, positioning himself behind the upright bum cheeks of the gorgeous girl, kneeling so that his balls swung across Sasha's face, he made ready to plunge his prick into Sally from the rear.

His proud prick slipped under Sally's bottom as his

uncovered knob probed the entrance to her loveslit. Sasha was now being given a worm's eye view and he raised his head to lick at Sally's stiff little clitty that gleamed long and erect through her black pubic bush. Radleigh and I then joined in the fun by each sucking one of Sally's large nipples which made her writhe and twist so much that poor Conrad could hardly keep his prick in her lusciously slippery pussey.

This frenetic activity now made its effect known on Sasha whose prick at last began to rise. Sally brushed his rising cock with her cheek and caressed his balls with her moist lips as Radleigh and I took our mouths away from her titties and concentrated on each other. He padded behind me, teasing my bare bottom with his big cock as I reached behind me and tickled his balls.

Perhaps it was the sight of Conrad fucking Sally so beautifully from behind that gave me the idea, but I too wanted to be taken from the rear so I knelt on the carpet and motioned Radleigh to take me doggy-fashion. He moved into position and I guided his prick (which was not very thick but of a good length) right into my sopping cunt. He set about riding me at a furious pace, his tempo so fast that I almost fell forward. Radleigh grabbed me round the waist and found my clitty straight away, massaging it skilfully while nibbling my earlobe. I shouted out that I was about to spend so he gave a final huge lunge and his hot creamy spunk shot straight up into me as my own juices began to flow.

Molly had been busy bringing the maid to orgasm but now she wanted a cock in her cunney instead of a tongue. She had to wait until Conrad had recovered (aided by a glass of iced champagne mixed with fresh orange juice, a concoction of which I thoroughly approve). Neither Radleigh nor Sasha were able to offer Molly any comfort but the younger man was in peak physical condition and he valiantly offered his services to my lovely cousin.

But could Conrad rise to the occasion yet again? Molly squeezed his cock and rubbed his shaft up and down in so expert a fashion that his cock was soon jutting proudly out from between his muscular lean thighs. He placed Molly on her back on the divan and we all crowded round to see this most voluptuous liaison. He held her hips up off the velvet as he knelt between them, taking all the liberties he desired, kissing and sucking the nipples of her divinely formed breasts, handling and squeezing her bum cheeks, frigging her erect little clitty until, drawing up his grand tool, he rubbed her pussey lips until she begged for the handsome lad to push the ruby head firmly between them.

'Ahhh! Ahhhh! Conrad! What a fine fellow you are,' she gasped, heaving her hips upwards to match his downward thrusts. 'That's right, push harder now, further in, further in!'

Her bottom responded to every shove. As he drove home, his lusty cock slapped in and out between her cunney lips. How they enjoyed each other's bodies; they clung to each other in ecstasy, the lips of her cunt clinging to his cock, holding on and protruding in a most luscious manner at each withdrawing motion, but it could not last too long and I noted the tell-tale tremor in Conrad's spine as he stabbed forward into Molly's pussey, spurting his spunk deep inside her. Molly's cries of fulfilment echoed around the room as her cunt milked his cock of love juice as they sank down together.

We stayed the night at Berbeck Lodge and I must confess that before exhaustion overtook us, we indulged in some more fine fucking which I enjoyed very much. But in the morning – not too early, as we did not take breakfast until half past ten – we drove back to Sasha's cottage and spent the rest of the day quietly. And as you know, dear diary, Molly and I actually spent the night in one room and the two men spent the night in theirs because we were all so tired from our games with Radleigh Berbeck that we needed to refresh ourselves for the journey we were to take at midday.

We are bound for Coney Island to see what Conrad says is the most attractive of all summer amusements, the great show and circus of Phineas T. Barnum, the foremost show-man of his age. I am looking forward immensely to this outing and will record my impressions as soon as possible, diary, in your pages.

August 22nd, 1884

On the train journey to Coney Island we met up with two friendly young men with whom Conrad was acquainted. Their names were Douglas Walker and David Taylor and they were studying at the great University of Harvard, which is situated in the town of Cambridge, Massachusetts. They were both medical students, engaged in some form of research, and we arranged to dine with them later in the week when we were back in Manhattan.

However, on to the circus! How can I best describe the scene? Well, to begin with, there were enormous posters everywhere, posters quite big enough to hide the front of a railway station and graphic enough to excite the wonder and amazement of everyone who saw them.

The day before, there had been a grand parade through the streets and we were amongst the many thousands of people who flocked towards the showground. David Taylor informed me that working men saved up their funds religiously for Barnum's visit which is regarded as one of the principal occurrences of the year. The roads leading to the grounds were as crowded as Cheapside on Lord Mayor's Day, and the throng entered an awning vast enough to cover six acres. Inside there was a side show of 'living curiosities', an exhibition of wild beasts and a three-ring circus.

The 'living curiosities' were quite repulsive but I enjoyed the exhibition, which contained no less than eighteen elephants. Within the circus, performances were proceeding in each of the three rings at one and the same time – here a bare-backed rider turning somersaults on his steed, there three elephants executing evolutions at command, beyond an acrobat terrifying the spectators with daring feats on the trapeze.

'This place must take a mint of money,' muttered Conrad as we watched the athletic young trapeze artist risk life and limb fifty feet above our heads. 'There must be some ten thousand people here all paying a fifty cents admission charge and in the evening the whole performance is repeated.'

'Well, there are quite a few people on the payroll,' said Conrad. 'And it must cost a considerable amount to feed all the animals. Also, the circus cannot tour during the winter months and the whole show is laid up in Bridgeport, Connecticut. Still, I do agree that Mr Barnum must have earned a fortune.'

We strolled around, enjoying the spectacle until six o'clock when we left to take the train back to Long Branch. We agreed that it had been a most pleasant outing but I noticed that Molly had been somewhat quieter than usual and I asked her if all was well with her.

'Yes, I'm quite all right, Jenny,' she answered a little absent-mindedly. 'If I appear somewhat thoughtful it is because of Conrad's nice young friend Douglas Walker who we met this morning.'

'Oh dear, I hope he was not impolite,' said Conrad.

'No, no, far from it,' said Molly. 'The truth is that Douglas reminds me of my first lover. Coincidentally, his name was Douglas, too, and we were both sweet sixteen. Douglas was the vicar's son and we used to meet every Sunday afternoon.'

'So your virginity was taken by a man of the cloth?' inquired Sasha.

'Not exactly, for Douglas was quite irreligious and had no desire to enter the ministry. I have not heard from him now for some three years but in his last letter he talked of going abroad to seek his fortune.

'However, he did take my virginity. I remember the afternoon well. It was a sultry summer day and we were lying out on the lush grass of a field near our home. I had let Douglas kiss me before and we had put our tongues in each other's mouths. I had let him caress my breasts and even unbutton my blouse and play with my hardening nipples. But we never passed that love-making stage, though I had been sorely tempted to stroke the bulge in his trousers.

'Perhaps it was the heat that made me lose control when he gently slid a hand up my skirt and began to rub my pussey which was already dampening under his touch. I made no move to stop him and indeed assisted him by arching my back as he pulled down my drawers. I felt for the bulge which throbbed underneath my hand as he rubbed harder against my wet bush and soon he had two fingers in my untried, though soaking, cunney and we were kissing wildly à la française.

'He then unbuttoned his fly and freed his cock, the first I had ever seen and I admired the thick shaft with its fiery uncapped head. "Rub it up and down for me, Molly," he whispered and, nothing loath, I followed his instruction. It felt so good, so invigorating holding this meaty prick in my warm hand that, allied with all the finger-fucking and caressing which was taking place, I desperately wanted Douglas to fuck me properly.

'But the clever young rogue was wise beyond his years and his fingers quickened as my juices began to flow freely over his hand. He gently pushed my head downwards with the other hand and as he had correctly surmised, I could not resist his hard, stiff cock standing so proudly just inches from my lips. I moved myself round to enable my mouth to wholly engulf it then moved my lips up and down the length, licking and sucking this throbbing truncheon which pulsed and quivered away under my touch.

'He felt his climax approaching but, thoughtfully, not knowing whether I wished to swallow his cream, did not attempt to spend in my mouth. Instead, he rolled me over on to my back and after carefully parting my throbbing cunney lips, slowly entered me so I could feel each ribbed muscle as first his helmet and then his thick shaft passed deep into my welcoming love-box.

'He started to pump away and moving one hand over my trembling buttocks, he started to tickle my clitty from behind. His cock felt enormous and I humped my hips to meet his every thrust as he fucked me hard and fast. When I started to spend I squealed with pleasure, and a few seconds later he jetted great blobs of warm spunk into my pussey.

'We lay exhausted for a while and then Douglas slid his hand across to caress my firm breasts. "I've always loved your titties; they are so big and soft," he sighed, pinching my nipples to electric life. He began to lick my nips but this time I was the one to push his head back so that he lay back in a supine fashion to await my sweet attack.

'I moved my mouth down his lean body, leaving a wake of feathery kisses. My tongue soon met the object of my desire and his smooth pink prick was already standing stiffly to attention as I flicked my tongue out to taste the little pool of white froth that had gathered at the slit. "Suck me, please, Molly," gasped the young rascal, and I opened my lips and engulfed his whole cock. It nudged the back of my throat and I began sucking and sliding my lips up and down his plump shaft. My fingers toyed with his swinging balls and his pubic hair tickled my nose. Oh my, it was heavenly to have his cock in my mouth! When I felt him tremble with the excitement of a further spend, I held his balls and greedily swallowed every drop of his copious emission of hot sperm.

'And when, so to speak, he had caught his second wind, Douglas slid down my body and spread my thighs wide and with his flashing tongue he licked out all the sopping sex juices that had accumulated there during our love-making, which enabled me to experience a further delicious orgasm.'

There was a momentary silence as we digested Molly's erotic confession. Hearing friends' stories of their first sexual experiences always excites me so I asked Conrad if he would regale us with the account of how he lost his virginity. He smiled and said: 'Oh, I do not wish to bore the company with all the sordid details.'

'No, no, do go on, Conrad, tell us all,' we chorused.

'Are you certain you want me to tell all?' he teased, as we all repeated our request to hear of his sexual deflowering.

'Oh, do tell us, Conrad,' said Molly persuasively. 'I feel like hearing a good horny story. We won't tell tales, and if you excite us as much as I am sure you will, Jenny and I will suck your cock together, won't we, Jenny?'

Well, why not, I thought as I nodded my head in agreement.

This was all the extra encouragement Conrad needed, so we settled back in our seats to listen to Conrad's account of how he first crossed the sexual Rubicon.

'Although my parents were financially secure,' he began, 'I was never cossetted overmuch by having a posse of servants at my beck and call. As our two lovely English guests now know, this is not really the style here in America, except amongst the hugely wealthy commercial barons in New York, who feel it necessary to ape the ways of the Old World.

'However, we did employ two parlourmaids, and, as is often the case here, both were young girls who wished to improve their English. One was German, a dark-haired quite attractive girl named Helga and the other was Bibi, a most delightful creature who hailed from Sweden. Tragically, her parents had both died in a terrible fire when she was very young and she had been brought up in a small village not far from Stockholm by a childless couple who had been friends of her late parents. While they had been most kind and affectionate to Bibi, she had always wanted to travel, so with their blessing, she left Sweden for America just days after she reached the age of eighteen.

'She spoke some English that she had learned at school but, being unskilled and wanting to improve her mastery of the language, she found employment with my family as a parlourmaid about three months before my own sixteenth birthday.

'Ah, but what a girl was Bibi! Well, I should phrase that in the present tense as happily she is still very much alive and I am glad to say, enjoying life here in the land of the free. She was slightly taller than average with a mop of bright blonde curls which set off to perfection a cheeky little face with large blue eyes that fairly sparkled with promise. Her slim, athletic frame and light complexion were shown off delightfully by her maid's black dress. My eyes would gaze longingly at her perfectly formed breasts that jutted out like two firm globes. Every night I would think of Bibi as I lay in bed with my rock-hard cock in my hand. I only had to rub the shaft for about half a minute before the spunk shot out of my prick but, of course, this relief was only temporary and no satisfactory substitute for my raging lust.

'Well, two nights before my sixteenth birthday, my parents had been invited to Boston for a ball given by John O'Connor, the property magnate, and this meant that I would be alone in our mansion with only Bibi and old Bailey the butler, for Helga had been given leave to visit her friends in Brooklyn for a few days.

'Mrs White, the cook, did not live in and so after dinner I sat alone in the drawing room, reading a newspaper. Bailey the butler came in and asked permission to lock up as he was suffering from a bad headache and I readily gave him permission to retire to his room. I was quite tired myself so I decided to go upstairs and read in bed. Hidden in my wardrobe was a copy of a magazine of French postcards I had purchased from a schoolfriend and truth to tell, I could not wait to feast my eyes on those lovely undraped lovelies whose pictures would swell my cock up like a steel rod.

'I undressed quickly and took out the magazine from its hiding place in a wardrobe drawer. It was a warm night so I lay on the bed naked and, as I thumbed my way through the magazine, drinking in the sight of those tittivating young girls wearing very little or indeed nothing at all, my cock soon rose up majestically, stiffening to attention and demanding to be exercised. One picture in particular, of a shapely girl lying on her back completely bare with her legs apart fingering the lips of her pussey which were only partially hidden by a fine growth of cunney hair, had me panting away as I rubbed my cock up to bursting point.

'The fantasy of running my hands over that luscious body, of handling those delicious titties and then of placing my hot, throbbing prick in her cunt . . . it was all too much and my spunk was soon spurting up in fierce spurts as that wonderful feeling surged through my body.

'Of course at that tender age, after only a brief respite, one is ready to begin all over again and as I turned the page to look at the magnificent big bare breasts of one Mademoiselle Estelle of Quentonne (a little village north west of Paris which I determined to visit as soon as I could cross the Atlantic!) my cock swelled up again and was as stiff as a poker as I gently caressed it slowly.

'I was so wrapped up in this lustful activity that I did not hear my bedroom door open or see Bibi enter. But when I looked up there she was, smiling broadly as she licked her lips.

'I was so flustered and taken aback that I hastily dropped the magazine and my cock shrank down to near limpness. "Oh, what has happened to your cock?" asked Bibi with a little frown. "This must be corrected instantly. I know how to make it stand up again." And her lovely hand grasped and squeezed my cock, slowly tossing me off as my cock's stiffness rapidly returned to its former length and strength.

'"You have such a lovely cock, Master Conrad," murmured Bibi. "Perhaps you would like to fuck me as your sixteenth birthday present?" Wouldn't I just!!! Trembling with excitement, I could only nod my acceptance and immediately this delicious girl undressed in front of my delighted eyes. She was stark naked as she walked towards me, her firm, uptilted breasts looked up pertly as our mouths met and my hands ran over her hard, engorged nipples and her own hand encased my throbbing shaft which bucked uncontrollably in her sweet grasp. She pulled her face away from mine as we crashed down upon the bed and pushed my head down between her legs to give me my first view of a real life naked pussey.

'Bibi was justly proud of her pussey for her thighs were full and proportionately made, with a mass of silky blonde hair between them that formed a perfect veil over her pouting little slit. As we writhed in each other's arms, my cock began to leap and prance about as it sought an entrance into the hospitable retreat that awaited. The dear girl sensed how badly I wanted her so without further ado she whispered: "Come, Conrad, you are about to enjoy your first fuck!" It did not occur to me at the time to wonder how quickly she had mastered the vernacular (in fact it was the roguish young Jonathan, the coachman's twenty-year-old son who had initiated Bibi into the joys of fucking and who had taught her some everyday expressions that were never taught during the lessons she attended at Mr Kirby's School of English on Forty Second Street!) but at that time, nothing mattered in the whole world except getting my cock in Bibi's cunney.

'Bibi lay on her back with her legs apart as, quivering with anticipation, I lowered myself upon her. I moaned as she took hold of my cock and guided it firmly into her juicy wet quim. Perhaps it was fortunate that only minutes before I had spent through my own solo efforts, for instead of rushing in and out in a mad frenzy, I thrust my yearning cock in her pussey at a slower rate, going right in and then withdrawing all but the tip of my prick before plunging in again to the full. This had the desired effect upon Bibi whose bottom began to roll around as she arched her back, working her cunt back and forth against the ramming of my thick young cock. She loved to fuck and was enjoying my very first efforts in fucking as she gasped: "Oh, lovely, really lovely, Conrad. Ah, those long powerful strokes and – oh, yes – now, Conrad, now, make me spend! Ram your cock into me, shoot your spunk! I want it all!"

'I shuddered with pleasure as I knew that the moment of supreme pleasure was nigh. I sheathed my cock so fully inside her pussey that my balls nestled against her chubby bum cheeks. Then faster and faster I slid my cock in and out until I cried out with sheer unadulterated joy as powerful squirts of creamy spunk exploded into her, on and on, until the last faint dribblings oozed out of my now shrunken prick. I withdrew from her cunt, rolling off her to lie beside my first lover, panting with pleasure and some little exhaustion. But I had done it! I had fucked a girl, a feat I knew that none of my friends had yet achieved. And oh, what a marvellous feeling had coursed through my veins, so much, much more satisfying than tossing off.

'It's almost nine years ago since that eventful evening, but it is one I shall always remember with delight and gratitude. Bibi had given me the best birthday present any boy could ask for and I enjoyed another three or four fucks until she left us to marry young Jonathan (who was totally unaware, of course, of Bibi's little escapades with me) and they went out West. I am delighted to be able to finish this narrative by telling the company that Bibi is now enjoying domesticity as the wife of the Mayor of Bickler, Texas, a fine little railway town where she and Jonathan are living very comfortably. First love can be idyllic or disastrous. Thanks to my kind Swedish Bibi, my initiation into manhood was marvellous. We have no glasses to toast her, so I will end by saying, Bibi, I salute you!'

There followed a short silence, broken only by the clackety-clack of the carriage wheels along the track and then Molly said slowly: 'That must have been a wonderful experience, Conrad. Bibi is surely a very special woman.'

'Indeed she is,' agreed Conrad. 'She remains to this day generous, though not undiscriminating, with her favours and being married does not inconvenience her because young Jonathan turned out to be a voyeur who likes nothing better than to watch his wife being fucked by other men.'

'How perfectly dreadful!' I exclaimed.

'Don't be too hasty to judge them, Jenny. Remember that it takes all sorts to make up our world. Live and let live is a wise motto,' chipped in Sasha, wagging his finger at me.

'I agree and, so long as both partners enjoy what they are doing, I can see nothing wrong, although I must say I find it all very strange. I would not want my wife to be fucking other men, let alone watch her participate in such activities,' said Conrad.

'So she is still fucking with friends?' Molly inquired.

'Just so,' Conrad answered. 'She is, as you might say, the good time had by all.'

We laughed at his clever quip and Molly and I snuggled up on each side of the virile young man and, as I kissed him, Molly's naughty hand began to unbutton his trousers.

'We promised you a double sucking and we don't break promises, do we, Jenny?' said Molly, as she delicately undid Conrad's belt and getting down on her knees in front of him, she pulled his trousers and drawers down to his ankles, releasing his stiffening cock which rose perceptibly before my eyes. Molly grasped the shaft with both hands, capping and uncapping the fiery red dome before her head swooped down, caressing and licking his knob, teasing and tantalising his balls with her fingers.

'Leave some for me!' I cried, as I too sank to the floor, cupping his hairy ballsack in my hands. My tongue flicked out to moisten his throbbing shaft as Molly continued to suck lustily on his knob. We then switched over and as I took over tonguing the mushroom dome, I tickled his balls with my fingernails and his frothy white spunk jumped out and cascaded into my mouth. It poured down my throat, so that I did not need to swallow once.

'But can you still come again after your first spend?' inquired Molly, whose pussey, no doubt like mine, was throbbing with unslaked desire. She slipped expertly out of her clothes. Her well-rounded breasts with their large yet pert nipples looked so inviting that I wanted to take them into my mouth, but I resisted this temptation to take Conrad's semi-stiff cock between my lips. I sucked hard and felt the shaft all the way back in my throat.

But then I felt a similar hardness against my cheek and I opened my eyes to see it was Sasha's stiff prick rubbing itself urgently against my face. Not unreasonably, he felt the need to participate in our frolics. Well, one must aid the needy as well as the greedy, so I pulled Conrad's cock out of my mouth and turned to Sasha's thick prick, flicking the hard, pink head with my hungry tongue. It was like following a bouncing ball. I had to take hold of it to get it in my mouth and I went from one to the other until Sasha gushed powerful squirts of seed into my mouth which I gulped down. I enjoy the taste of sperm which I find most invigorating.

Molly's eyes shone when she saw how Conrad's cock had hardened to perfection and she bent over, putting her hands on the seat and opening her legs so that her lovely bum faced Conrad's throbbing rod.

'I feel like the pool player with a problem,' muttered Conrad, stroking his cock.

'Why?' I asked.

'I don't know whether to go for the pink or the brown,' he replied. 'But let's start here.' He slid his cock into Molly's pussey from behind and reached around with his hand, circling her clitty with his long fingers.

'Ooooooh! That's glorious,' yelled Molly with abandon. 'More, more, pump your lovely cock into me, Conrad. Oooh! Yes, yes, yes!' And perhaps it was the rocking of the train that gave Conrad's cock that extra impetus, but Molly came almost immediately after he began fucking her and his own exquisite spend came very soon after, flooding her dripping pussey with his love juice.

August 29th, 1884

I was invited to a house-party last night by the charming young medical student David Taylor. We travelled to our destination by means of the elevated railway. These railways constitute one of the most striking features of that remarkable city. Metal pillars, erected at the edge of the pavement or in the centre of broad avenues, and standing some twenty feet high, support the lines along which passenger trains are driven at intervals of five or six minutes.

The long straight streets of the city are, of course, peculiarly suited for this strange mode of locomotion. Passengers who use it can look down upon the heads of the pedestrians below, or into the sitting rooms and bedrooms of the houses they are passing. Access to the numerous stations is obtained by flights of iron steps at the corners of the streets.

The quick and cheap transport that the railway provides is of immense value, but I must note that the appearance of the thoroughfares has been sadly marred by the lines. Some streets, where junctions are formed, look like tunnels. It was breathtaking, however, to cross the Brooklyn Bridge which was only opened last year by President Arthur. This stupendous suspension bridge cost more than fifteen million dollars and was rightly judged by M. de Lesseps as the greatest engineering triumph of the age.

'Tell me about the people who are giving the party tonight, David?' I asked as we walked along in the cool evening air.

'Oh, of course you have never met Michael and Clare, have you, Jenny? He is a wealthy banker but they really are an odd couple.'

'In what way?'

'Well, it is somewhat indelicate, but I could illustrate what I mean through an anecdote.'

'Please do, David,' I said. 'I am no prude.'

'Very well, then. It really is a strange story, but I assure you that it is absolutely true.

'About three months ago, my girlfriend Sally and I were invited to dine with Michael and Clare. However, I knew that I would be delayed so Sally said she would meet me there. I arrived some half an hour after the time I knew Sally had probably arrived and to my astonishment the front door was on the latch. I opened it and closed it behind me, but there appeared to be no-one else in the house. The silence was quite eerie.

'Then I heard a noise from upstairs so, thinking there may be thieves about, I tip-toed up the stairs only to hear the sound of muffled giggling from one of the main bedrooms. My first thought was to burst in as I assumed that Sally was being fucked by Michael, especially when I heard his voice saying: "You are sure that I am not hurting you, my dear?" But just as I was about to confront them I heard Clare's clear tones saying, "Lie back, Sally and I will suck your cunt while you suck Michael's cock."

'All was revealed! There was obviously a sexual *menage à trois* taking place and when I heard the juicy slurping sounds emanating from the bedroom, I could well imagine Clare sucking Sally's pussey, bringing her slowly to orgasm. Then I thought of Sally sucking lustily on Michael's prick and the thought excited me greatly. I unbuttoned my flies to release my swelling cock and as the sounds of fucking became more heated, I began to toss myself off.

'I was near the peak of pleasure when the bedroom door opened and out strode Sally, completely naked, making her way to the bathroom. She had not seen me but I walked into the bedroom and Michael said: "Ah, David, we have been expecting you. Take off your clothes and join in the fun. Would you like to fuck Clare?"

'I overcame my initial embarrassment and slipped out of

my clothes. I lay down on top of Clare and Michael took hold of my cock and directed it to the edge of Clare's cunney. "In you go," he said cheerily. "Clare's pussey is sopping wet as Sally and I have both been sucking it."

'I sank my cock into her warm, welcoming snatch and quickly shot my load of boiling sperm inside her. I rolled off her and now Sally returned to the fray, armed with a long black dildo. She and Clare entwined themselves into a most passionate embrace, their lips hard against each other. Clare began to fuck Sally's slit with the dildo, a sight that again I found extraordinarily exciting.

'My cock rose up to a quite giant erection and Michael began to rub my cock with his left hand and his own stiff prick with his right hand. Clare continued to slip the dildo in and out of Sally's pussey but she now turned her attention to my cock, which she licked and sucked. Sally was now positioned on all fours and pushed out her firm, young bum-cheeks towards me.

'I rubbed my cock between her buttocks and then slowly inserted my cock into her pussey from behind. Gripping her hips, I pulled Sally towards me with every inward thrust and pushed her away with each outward movement so she jerked back and forth which gave her great pleasure. She lasted only a few minutes of this vigorous onslaught until she cried out, with delight: "I'm spending, yes, I'm spending, oh, oh, oh!" and, with a great shudder, she collapsed on the pillow as I too reached my climax, spunking hard into her eager cunt before falling on top of her. We continued to fuck until midnight, when we dressed and refreshed ourselves with the cold collation the servants had put out.

'I haven's seen them since and indeed I haven's seen Sally for some six weeks now, as she is with her parents in Chicago,' he concluded rather forlornly.

'Goodness,' I exclaimed. 'So you have not enjoyed a good fuck for all that time?'

'That is the unfortunate case,' he replied glumly.

'Perhaps your luck will change tonight,' I said and to

cheer him up, I gave him a nice, wet kiss full on the lips. We were now at the gate of Michael and Clare's imposing house but David stopped just inside the front garden and taking me in his arms returned my kiss with real passion. I opened my mouth to welcome his tongue and he reached for my bosoms. I pressed my left breast hard against his hand but then swiftly broke away. 'Let's see what kind of party this is, David. After all, we may not want to return together.'

'Gee,' said David. 'And I thought you English girls were so reserved.'

'So we are,' I murmured, giving his ear a playful little nip. 'No guarantees are given and you must take your chance. Anyhow, Sally may be here tonight.'

'No, she has gone up-state with her parents. But even if she were here, I would much rather fuck you.'

'Well, thank you for the compliment. I cannot tell you who I will fuck with tonight, if I fuck at all, but I think I can say that, at this stage, you are at the head of the queue.'

As you know, dear diary, I rather enjoyed the party. There were several medical people there, including Doctor Lucy Danielle, the brilliant physician, who treated President Arthur when he contracted pneumonia last autumn. I hope there will be far more women taking up medicine as a career as I believe that they would prove an exceptional boon to our sex. At present, we have to tell our troubles to men who respond with a varied degree of concern and expertise, which is not entirely their fault for how can a man know, for example, just how a period pain feels or what goes through a woman's mind and body during the process of childbirth?

After depositing our coats and greeting our genial hosts, we were ushered into the somewhat ornately furnished drawing room where some twenty or so people were clustered round the attractive Doctor Danielle. Though now in her late forties, she was still an attractive and pretty lady. She was holding the floor in a general discussion on intimate medical matters, which I found most illuminating.

149

'Tell me, Doctor Danielle,' said a swarthy-skinned young man. 'I've just begun to bed a lovely girl who is fabulous between the sheets, and she has found a most unusual position for intercourse. After I insert my penis in her pussey, she keeps one leg on the bed and then lifts the other one right up over my shoulder so she is practically doing the "splits". She says it makes her come more easily. Is there any harm in this practice?'

'No, no, not at all,' laughed Doctor Danielle, taking a huge gulp of red wine from the glass she was fondling in her hands. 'If any position can be found that gives pleasure and does not strain the body, then it is most unlikely that any damage will be done.

'As to your girlfriend, well, jolly good luck to her. You see, Edwin, different positions of the legs create different pressures inside the vaginal area and the position you have described makes the penis seem even larger and enables the very deepest penetration to be made. I would guess that her cunney feels tight to you when she takes up this position, right?'

'Quite right,' said Edwin gratefully. 'So may we carry on fucking?'

'By all means, my dear fellow. It's fine exercise and far better for you than smoking or drinking.'

'You're a fine one to talk, Doctor, swigging down that wine,' said a tall young girl standing on the edge of the group.

'Unfortunately, my lover has gone to give a lecture at Brooklyn Medical College tonight, so I have to make do with a substitute pleasure,' she gaily replied.

'Fair enough,' said the tall girl. 'But while I agree with the advice you gave Edwin, I do think that traditional ways are often the best. Certainly they should not be discarded simply because they are old-fashioned.

'Indeed, when Edwin was fucking me earlier this year, he only wanted to try various different positions which is why, incidentally, I was surprised that he was anxious about his new lover's preferences for unusual love-making. Why, we tried it standing up, me on top, sitting on a chair, my bending over the bed doggy-fashion and others.

'But frankly, Doctor, I honestly prefer the straightforward method, with him on top of me on a springy, comfortable mattress in a warm bed. Am I too inhibited, perhaps, for really I find it the most enjoyable way to fuck?'

'I don't want to give the impression that old-fashioned ways are in any way wrong. Most couples end up making love in the ways that both find the most comfortable. This may take some form of compromise, perhaps one night the man's way and the next night, the woman's way.

'And I do agree with you, it so happens. The man on top, girl underneath is my own particular favourite and, indeed, all over the world it is the most popular sexual position. But variety is the spice of life, so they say, and I think you must try alternative ways to fuck, because who knows what delights there may be in store for you. Some new idea – sucking his cock and swallowing his spunk, for example – might prove to be sheer bliss for you both.

'And anyhow, experimentation staves off boredom in a relationship, though your man must always respect your views – and you, his – and neither must force each other to try anything that feels uncomfortable. I mean, I have never been able to take a cock up my arse, though I know that some girls actually prefer a prick in the bottom to a cock in the cunt. Still, it takes all sorts, as the proverb has it.'

'It does take all sorts, Doctor, you are quite right there,' said a handsome, older man standing just behind me. 'Why, my girlfriend has the most fabulous bosom I have ever had the good fortune to fondle. Her breasts are beautifully plump with exquisitely formed pink aureoles and high-tipped strawberry nipples that stiffen up like two miniature pricks when I stroke them.

'I want to lick them, suck them, rub my face against them, but can you believe that she does not enjoy this and though she allows me to play with her titties, she does not respond and simply sits there with a bored expression on her face.'

'Dear me, that's quite extraordinary,' said Doctor Danielle thoughtfully. 'The breasts are usually most sensitive to the touch and most girls are stimulated by having their breasts kissed and fondled. Possibly, this girl fears that her lovers are only interested in her breasts and not in other parts of her body.

'My suggestion is that you show appreciation of her hair, her bottom, her hairy grotto with the pink slit pouting out from the mossy growth, and if you do this, my guess is that she will come to enjoy the attention being paid to her titties as much as you evidently do.'

This interesting conversation was interrupted by the Negro butler who announced in sonorous tones that dinner was about to be served, and we all trooped off towards the dining-room.

After a delicious dinner, David, myself and the other guests retired back to the drawing-room. The chairs had been arranged in a semi-circle and the lights had been dimmed, except for two powerful lamps which shone brightly in the centre of the room, now lit like a miniature stage.

'What happens now?' I asked David.

'It's Michael and Clare's after-dinner entertainment,' he replied, as our host began to strike up a jolly tune on the piano.

Almost immediately, a lithe Negro youth came into the room dressed solely in a buttoned-up red smoking jacket that just covered his bum. David whispered that his name was Joshua and that he was the seventeen-year-old son of the butler and his wife who looked after the household's laundry. And then to a spattering of polite applause, a dusky girl of about the same age stepped into the spotlight. Her name was Iris and she was Joshua's girlfriend. She also appeared to wear nothing but a smoking jacket only hers was light blue in colour, and together they began to dance sensuously to the accompaniment of Michael's accomplished piano playing.

I admired their graceful movement as their long legs swivelled effortlessly in time with the music. Then, in a simultaneous movement, the two dancers shucked off their robes and their glistening, proud bodies were revealed in all their naked glory to our admiring eyes. Iris's skin was the colour of milky coffee and her pretty, rounded breasts were well separated, each looking a little away from the other, each a globe of perfection with two rosebud points which she stroked up until they stood out like miniature little red soldiers. Her smooth, flat belly was set off by the thick black bush of curls that graced her pouting little pink slit, from which I saw that her tiny clitty was already protruding from between her cunney lips.

Josh was slightly darker in complexion with broad shoulders and a deep, manly chest, which was yet quite smooth and hairless. His firm muscles showed well in all his movements, for there was little soft fat on his torso. But what took my eye, and that of all the spectators, I am sure, was his amazingly long, thick prick which was standing just slightly erect giving us a fair view of his velvety, wrinkled ballsbag, which swung as he pirouetted around the floor.

Iris stood still in a classical pose whilst Josh knelt in front of her, his long, muscular arms like perfect black marble, his hands caressing her gorgeous breasts. His cock began to rise majestically upwards until his shaft was flat up against his belly, his knob end almost uncovered. The impudent girl hoisted Josh up by his shoulders so that they were locked standing in a tight embrace, with only his magnificent thick cock between them. She slid down her hand to grasp his cock and gave the shaft a vigorous rub.

Josh ran his fingers through her curly bush as she opened her legs wide to enable him to insert three fingers between her cunney lips. He worked his fingers gently in her cunt and she moaned with pleasure as he increased the tempo. In a flash they were both down on the floor in a 'sixty nine',

Josh on his back and Iris with her bum just over his face, leaning forward to lower her mouth on his throbbing cock as he parted her bum cheeks and began to lick and lap at her pussey.

At his tender age, Josh could not be expected to hold back his excitement and Iris must have felt that he was about to come for she suddenly stopped sucking and grasped the monster shaft with both hands. With a cry, the boy jetted out a fountain of frothy spunk which fell partly on his belly and partly on Iris's face. She licked up the spunk from his belly and sucked out the last drops from his cock which was slowly losing its stiffness, the purple head disappearing under the foreskin.

I was so engrossed in watching this exhibition fucking that I accidently knocked over a glass of water off a side-table, though fortunately most of the water went over my hands and none on my clothes.

Hastily, I apologized to our hostess but Clare generously put me at my ease by saying that no damage was done. 'However, as a forfeit, why don't you dry your hands on Joshua's big black cock?' she said.

'Yes, go ahead,' chimed in her husband, who was still seated on the piano and I could not help noticing that his trouser buttons were undone. 'Josh won't mind, will you, boy?'

'No sir. Sure won't,' grinned Josh.

Should I or shouldn't I? To gain time for thought, I said to Michael: 'Do you know your flies are undone?'

'No, Jenny, but you hum it and I'll play it!' retorted the witty musician. 'Come on, dry your hands on Josh's cock. Let's have a vote. All in favour say "aye".'

'Aye!' bellowed the company as one, so being of a democratic persuasion, I felt that the choice had been made for me.

I strode out into the centre of the floor where Josh stood, still quite naked but with his huge cock at half-mast, so I reached down with both hands and fondled his prick which immediately began to swell in my hands. Slowly, I ran my fingers across the tip and over the purple head and my wet hands gave me the necessary lubricant to slide them up and down his shaft, capping and uncapping his knob as he gave little gasps of delight.

Then with both hands, I cupped his heavy balls and massaged them gently, lifting and separating each one. Then I grabbed his shaft with both hands, one on top of the other and began a sliding, rubbing action that sent Joshua into a moaning frenzy. I pumped and jerked his black cock, faster and faster, over the head, under the balls, then back along the shaft until he began humping into my palm. He gave a final push until, with a very loud groan, he squirted out jets of frothy white spunk as the company broke into wild applause.

I must admit that the party disintegrated into a bacchanalian affair after that, with the guests throwing off their clothes and indulging in every kind of fucking one could imagine. Every orifice was filled and in one memorable daisy chain I had a cock in my mouth, another up my bottom, with my hands tossing off two others for good measure.

However, David and I left the proceedings relatively early at just after midnight which was just as well, as an angry husband appeared soon after we left and found his errant wife sucking off Joshua while Michael was fucking her pussey from behind. He left immediately but returned soon afterwards with a shotgun and peppered Michael's arse with buckshot, though fortunately he was restrained before he could attempt to commit further grievous bodily harm upon his wife.

The police were called and the trial will give the lower class newspapers a field day. Only today I had a letter from Hal Freedman of the *New York Herald* – who you may remember, diary, I met briefly in Washington with Senator Easthouse – asking if it were true that I was at the news-making party. Candidly, I simply lied and said that I knew nothing about it.

But who could have told Hal Freedman about me? If it were Count Labotsky, I shall not enter his restaurant ever again but it would be totally out of character for Sasha to peach. More likely it was Ronnie Donne, as that randy dentist has been pestering me to visit his surgery for some days. I enjoyed fucking with him but it was strictly a one-off affair. I will confront Ronnie tomorrow and heaven help him if he is the culprit.

August 30th, 1884

After breakfast, I decided to visit Ronnie Donne, the randy dentist, to see whether he had sneaked about the goings-on at last night's party, though I doubted that Ronnie would be such a sneak. Still, it gave me an excuse to visit his surgery and as I had no cock to hand, so to speak, if Ronnie could convince me of his innocence, perhaps I would let him fuck me.

As it happened, dear diary, as well you know, I said my goodbyes to Molly who was visiting an old school friend who lived in Bootesville, Indiana. She would not be back for at least three days, but I was not to be lonely for long.

While I was reading the morning newspaper I became involved in an argument with a handsome young man who was engaged in a heated discussion about education for women. He was arguing that college education for girls was a waste of time and that women should concentrate only on dressmaking, cookery and other 'feminine occupations'.

I could not stay silent. 'You infer, sir,' I said calmly, 'that all women want to do is bear children, cook and clean for their families and be grateful that their menfolk come back to them every evening. Those ideas will soon be as dead as the dodo, Mr, er, Mr . . .'

'Tindall,' said the youth, smiling and offering his hand. 'Joseph Tindall at your service, Miss . . .'

'Everleigh, Jenny Everleigh from England,' I said. 'But really, you must be feeling inwardly most insecure if you believe that female emancipation from drudgery – for this is what we are talking about – will lead to the passing away of love between the sexes. Far from it, for the most gifted women are often those who possess the most lasting hold upon the passions.

'We must remove the artificial restraints that debar women from higher education (restraints that thankfully are not so severe here in this enlightened country than those unfortunately prevailing in my own native land). Women are already free to perform, if they choose, many kinds of important work.'

'They will not become improved women, but simply inferior men,' he argued.

'No, that is not so. Some mistakes will be made and blunders will occasionally result from the new freedom when it is obtained. But there is no more reason for fearing that women will, as a body, beset those professions for which they are manifestly unsuited than that free trade, would cause our Scottish cousins to produce wine instead of whisky.'

In the end I did manage to open his mind and in order to show that one could still be friendly after taking opposite sides in a heated discussion, I accepted his offer of a ride in his buggy down to Ronnie Donne's surgery.

Joe's girlfriend was otherwise engaged, so we were alone together as he drove steadily along through Central Park. I was wearing only a thin blouse under my jacket, for the sun was shining quite brightly, but a chilly breeze had suddenly blown up and my nipples were standing erect against the material of my blouse.

I think Joe noticed this as he pulled into a quiet lay-by and helped to cover me with a plaid blanket. With a flourish he brought out a silver hip-flask and poured out a measure of brandy. I thanked him and sipped the drink as he stood there smiling at me, flashing his white teeth. A tangle of wild, curly hair framed his rugged face and his laughing eyes seemed to question and tease all at once, holding my returned gaze, then glancing down to my hardened nipples.

'You aren't in too much of a hurry, are you, Jenny?' he asked.

'No, no, I can get there any time I want.'

'Well then, let's stay here a moment, ' said this good-looking young rogue as he stopped the horse and climbed into the cab with me.

'Have another drink, Jenny,' he said, handing me the glass and letting his arm graze my breasts.

'Joe, really, you should not do that, you might get into trouble.'

He laughed and said: 'Jenny, I think that I'm already in trouble.' I followed his gaze to his lap and saw a tremendous bulge straining against the grey cloth of his trousers. I lightly stroked the bulge and felt his prick jump under my touch.

'My lips are cold,' I murmured and, taking the hint, Joe puckered his mouth and placing it almost upon mine blew ever so gently on my lips, my eyes, my throat. A fierce sexual energy began to bubble up inside me as he brushed his lips against mine and gave me long, soft kisses that travelled down to the hollow of my neck.

I stroked the bulge in his crotch again as he tugged at his belt to release the catch. As he did so, I undid his buttons to see a truly magnificent naked cock, hard and erect, stand up out of a mass of thick black hair and to my delighted eyes it appeared that this thrilling monster organ simply begged to be sucked.

I bent forward and wet the cherry knob end with my tongue. My tongue ran the length of the marble hard shaft and then returned to the dome to catch a hot, sticky drip of spend that had formed at the little 'eye' on the knob. I ran my lips around the tip of his noble cock and then I opened my lips to accept its entrance. I sucked in as much of his throbbing shaft as I could, with one hand going under my skirt to finger my own hard clitty, while the other teased Joe's smallish but beautifully rounded balls.

'Stop, Jenny, or I'll come too quickly,' whispered my considerate lover. 'Let me pleasure you for a while.'

So I let go his cock and lay back as his hands dived under my skirt and pulled off my drawers. I lost sight of his head as it followed his hands under my skirt. Lifting my thighs either side of his head, he thrust his tongue between my wet pussey lips and began to circle around my dripping clitty. Almost of their own volition, my legs splayed wider as I sought to open myself even further to him. My stiff little clitty was drawn between Joe's lips which continued to quiver over my now frantic clitty.

I screamed out with delight, oblivious to the fact that people walking nearby might come by to investigate, as with a final flourish, he flicked his tongue once more over my clit and then placed it again between his lips and gently bit it. My body rocketed to the furthest heights of ecstatic madness in the sheer unashamed glory of my climax while Joe slurped my love juice into his mouth. Then he brought his face up to mine and licked my lips with his juice-coated tongue.

Leaning over me, he took hold of his fine prick and rubbed his rampant cock up and down my crack which sent me into new fits of wild abandon. I jerked my bum forward and I felt his delicious dome stretch my cunny lips apart to begin a truly stupendous fuck.

I clawed impatiently at his back and firm buttocks while his cock penetrated my cunney quite majestically, firmly yet gently. As he slid that fine prick in and out, stretching me to the limits, he steadied his balance, putting one hand under my head and the other under my hips. His gleaming cock, soaked in my juices, pounded in and out as I pleaded with him to push harder and deeper. My cunney was like a cello and Joe's prick was like the bow. Every long, exciting stroke raised the most ravishing melody throughout my body that could ever be experienced!

Then I felt the froth building up inside his balls and, oh, I exploded into an orgasm just as Joe plunged every last millimetre of his prick inside me, his balls banging against my bum as I arched my back to receive the spurts of jism that shot out of his shaft.

We collapsed, totally satiated but we soon composed ourselves and dressed quickly, as without doubt people would soon be coming past the stationary buggy. It's just as well that horses cannot talk or our fine stallion would have had a good story to tell. Anyhow, shortly afterwards, Joe dropped me outside Ronnie Donne's surgery and we promised to see each other again if time allowed, since I was still planning to take a trip to see Niagara Falls.

Ronnie was busy when I inquired if I could see him, so I sat down and enjoyed a cup of coffee with his receptionist, Diana, who confided to me that her newly wed husband was causing her some concern.

'Oliver is so jealous, Jenny,' she said. 'He is very loving but terribly suspicious. Why, he works nearby as a book-keeper at Blair's clothing store and almost always comes into the surgery to check that I am not having an affair with Ronnie or one of the patients.'

'You aren't, are you?' I asked.

'No, of course not, I only allow my husband to fuck me. Even before we were married I never had an affair with Ronnie, as neither of us believes in mixing business with pleasure. But even if I tell Oliver that I am having lunch with a girlfriend, he calls at the restaurant to see if I were telling the truth. If we go out together, he accuses me of looking at other men and sometimes accosts other men and tells them that they should not be looking at me! I have tried talking to him but nothing seems to work. I just don't know what to do about this insane jealousy.'

'I know what my old friend Doctor Lezaine would say,' I said. 'You must leave him until he realizes that while an element of jealousy and possessiveness makes up an element of a loving relationship, your husband's jealousy has made you both unhappy.

'Oliver needs medical aid to make him understand that the lack of confidence he shows in your behaviour is actually in proportion to how little he has in himself. Perhaps he can change his emotions by will alone, but I think he needs help to overcome this problem.'

'Thank you so much for your advice, Jenny,' she said. 'I'll contact our old family doctor who might be able to make Ollie see reason.'

'I certainly hope so,' I said. 'He is in other ways a good husband?'

'Indeed he is,' said Diana. 'He is in other ways, kind, affectionate and is very good at fucking. He sucks my quim beautifully and always tries to wait until I have spent before shooting his spunk into me.'

'He knows how to use his cock, Diana, and doesn't just bang in and out for a minute or two?'

'No, no. I adore his long stiff cock.'

'Then make him go to the doctor,' I advised. 'For a hard man is good to find.'

Ronnie and his patient came out of the surgery and, to my astonishment, the young man with the randy dentist was none other than Charles Nicholas, the officer who fucked me so exquisitely on board ship as I sailed across the Atlantic for this marvellous American vacation. He was not dressed in uniform but I would have recognised him even if he had been dressed as a Red Indian.

'Charlie! Charlie! Do you remember me?' I asked him excitedly.

'Of course I do! You are Jenny Everleigh. What a coincidence meeting you here. When are you coming home?'

'Next week, Charlie. Will you be on board?'

'I certainly will, for we are staying in New York on leave while the ship undergoes some refurbishment and repairs. Well, Jenny, how do you like America? Have you had an opportunity to see anything of the country outside New York?'

Suffice it to say that we chatted animatedly for some ten minutes and I accepted his invitation for luncheon so readily that I forgot the prime purpose of my visit to Ronnie Donne's! Still, I am sure that my dear big-cocked dentist was innocent of any unbecoming behaviour. As Molly was to comment later, Ronnie was no sneak and he was an old friend of Michael and Clare's, though he was one of their few close acquaintances who had never actually fucked her.

After our meal we strolled down Broadway to Charlie's

hotel and I did not demur when he asked me whether I would like to rest in his room for a while before going back to the Stuyvesant Club to begin packing for my trip to Niagara Falls tomorrow.

I knew what he meant – but I went! We were only in the room for as long as it took him to unlock the door and then his strong arms were clasped about me and we kissed passionately, the wet friction of his tongue making my whole mouth tingle with pleasure. I could fell him tugging at the buttons of my blouse so I assisted him in undoing them as I let my hands stray down to grasp his prick which felt as hard as a rock underneath his trousers. Charlie soon had me incredibly aroused and my whole body pulsed with excitement and my pussey was aching for further attention.

We undressed in record time and I gazed with undisguised longing at his thick stiff cock as he took off the last of his clothes. He stretched me out on the bed and knelt alongside, kissing my breasts and tummy and running his hands up and down my thighs. My excitement grew stronger and stronger and I clutched lovingly at his head, moaning my approval as he pressed his wet lips down onto my bushy mound.

The sensation of Charlie's mouth felt absolutely amazing and when I felt his tongue start licking at my clitty, I almost screamed with pleasure. I pushed my mound up against his sweet face and parted my legs as he began to lick and lap, his eager fingers prising open my pussey lips. He sank his finger slowly into my damp crack, making me gasp and tremble as he eased them deeper and deeper inside me.

Charlie's tongue and finger were thrilling me almost as if I had never been thrilled before. My clitty was tingling with a really intense excitement. He twisted his fingers round as he thrust them in, his knuckles pressing against the sides of my cunt and increasing my pleasure to an even higher pitch.

A searing wave of ecstasy built up inside me, growing more wonderful all the time. Charlie must have sensed my approaching climax because he lapped and sucked even more forcefully at my clitty and pushed his fingers in and out of my cunney even more quickly. As I felt myself spending I writhed wildly beneath him, holding his head firmly against my pussey with one hand while I squeezed at one of my nipples with the other. The fabulous pressure of Charlie's tongue and fingers kept me at the peak of pleasure for what seemed to be an incredibly long time.

Even when my climax eventually subsided, I still felt very ready to continue. More than anything, I wanted to return some of the pleasure he had afforded me so I urged him to lie back and knelt down at his feet. I then eased myself forward so that I too was lying down with his juicy cock just inches from my face.

I took hold of the ivory smooth shaft and holding the base in one hand, I flicked my tongue lightly round the smooth mushroom dome. I gradually eased it into my mouth, sucking harder as I did so and moving round my hand to caress his hairy ballsack. He clutched at my head as I squirmed with delight and began sucking his cock really frantically. His prick began throbbing against my tongue and then, whoosh, I sucked and swallowed a huge jet of creamy hot spunk that spilled into my mouth.

After a few minutes respite, I sucked Charlie's prick up to another fine erection and this time I wanted that big prick inside my cunney. I got on all fours and presented my bum to his delighted eyes.

'You have the most divine bum-cheeks, Jenny,' said Charlie. 'Now shall I fuck your arsehole or your cunt?'

'I would rather you didn't fuck my bum,' I replied.

'Fine, I just want to please you. You can imagine that we get enough bumhole on board ship but a nice juicy pussey is a far rarer commodity and it will be my great pleasure to cream it for you.'

And with those words he inserted his cock in my pussey from behind, clutching my tits in his hands and rubbing up the nipples until they stood up like little red stalks while he pumped away in and out of my saturated slit. Charlie seemed to know exactly how to please me most and the pressure and rhythm of his thrusts, together with the gorgeous way he fingered my clitty, brought me off at least three times before he shot his load of warm sperm up into my cunney. There was so much of it that the white jism dribbled down my legs and onto the sheet where it mingled with my own juices.

'I am sorry to say that we have stained your sheets,' I panted as we lay exhausted after our love-making.

'Your body was made for fucking, Jenny!' said Charlie. 'Now you are off to Niagara Falls and I won't see you again till we're sailing back to Britain. For the first time, I want my leave to fly by as quickly as possible, for I can hardly wait to see you again. Perhaps you will allow me to take you out when we get back home?'

'We'll have to see about that,' I said carefully. 'I did tell you that I have a boyfriend back home and that I am always true to him, darling, in my fashion. Yes, I'm always true to him, darling, in my way.'

The poor boy looked crestfallen so I kissed his insatiable cock which was already stirring and we spent another hour or so enjoying a most delicious bout of a fucking. What utter bliss!

'To Canada!' said the signpost. The appearance of this inscription on a fingerpost in the United States has a curious effect, especially as our American colonies are even more enormous in area than the territories of the Republic itself, extending as they do from the Atlantic to the Pacific, and from the Lakes to the Arctic Regions.

The fingerpost indicated, not the road to any particular town or village, but the road to one of the great dependencies of the British Crown. It was almost as if somebody had put up a signboard in Asia to point out, in an indefinite kind of way, the route to Africa. But the information conveyed by the fingerpost erected in the village of Niagara was correct enough. The street to which it directed the notice of a stranger led to the Suspension Bridge across the Niagara River, overlooking the wonderful cataracts.

The Niagara Falls, which everybody who visits America goes to see, have been so often described that I shall not myself add much to the literature of the subject. The best book I have read about the Niagara Falls was written by Professor Matthew Brendon-Cook F R S who also took some splendid photographs of the falls that illustrate his text admirably. I purchased a copy at Godfreys, a little bookshop in the Charing Cross Road.

However, I must not digress; the great chain of lakes which partly separates the United States from Canada penetrates the continent for considerably more than one thousand miles. These lakes fall one into the other, and so drain themselves through the Gulf of St Lawrence into the Atlantic Ocean. The elevation of Lake Erie is very much higher than that of Lake Ontario. Hence, the river that connects one lake with the other has to make a rapid descent from the higher to the lower level. Precipitated over precipices varying from one hundred and fifty to one hundred and sixty five feet, the Niagara River, near the village of that name, forms the Niagara Falls, down which over seven hundred thousand tons of water are projected every minute!

As the river approaches the precipice, it is divided by Goat Island. There are therefore two great falls, one called the American and the other the Horse Shoe or Canadian Falls. The latter is the more picturesque and the nearer one approaches, the more beautiful and awe-inspiring is the sight. The lovely colour of the water as it plunges into the abyss, the incessant and deafening roar it produces, the clouds of spray that are sent high up into the heavens, saturating everything in the neighbourhood as if it were exposed to continual rainfall, all make Niagara a spectacle to be remembered for ever.

But more extraordinary to my mind than even the falls themselves are the Whirlpool Rapids which are some three or four miles below them. After leaving the falls, the river pursues a tolerably placid career between the precipitous banks which enclose it, until a narrower channel is reached: then it rushes with such marvellous force and impetuosity through the gorge that an amazing phenomenon is produced. Apparently the impact of the water against the rocks on either side causes the river to bulge up in the middle, giving it an arched or rounded appearance.

It was here that Captain Webb (the man who first swam the English Channel) had his life literally crushed out by the awful forces he encountered in the foolish attempt to swim through the rapids and the whirlpool beyond.

Molly and I thoroughly enjoyed our visit, though the thought that poor Captain Webb met such an unnecessary end here saddened us for a while – especially as the gallant Captain was a distant relative of Molly's old friend, Doctor Dorothy Condron. Still, all in all, we had a wonderful outing aided by an excellent guide and the seasonal good weather.

September 7th, 1884

So here we are, dearest diary, back to England after a most wonderful vacation in the New World, a country that I see as a Greater Britain across the Atlantic.

I am writing this last epistle in this, my American diaries, in the stateroom provided for me by my sweet maritime lover, Charlie, who at this very moment is next to me in this luxurious bed.

He is fast asleep after one of the nicest fucks imaginable. He came to my bed exhausted after eight hours on duty but I soon managed to exite his lovely cock. Men so like to be teased. They adore having their necks nibbled and Charlie was no exception to the rule. I then ran my tongue around the outside of his ear and ran my long fingernails up the inside of his leg, stopping just short of his balls. It drove him to a frantic wildness and I so enjoyed playing with his big, rock-hard cock. We engaged in a short, intense bout of fucking and now poor Charlie is deep in the arms of Morpheus. But no doubt, I shall be able to arouse his interest after I have penned these final words in this record.

Little now remains to be added. I have neither uniformly praised nor uniformly disparaged the great country where I have so enjoyed myself. I have found in America, as I have found in England, many things that society would do better and be better without. If it were possible to take all the good one finds in America and add it to all the good one finds in England, one might be able to construct a nobler, more wholesome and more hopeful society than exists now in either country.

Certainly, I shall never forget the wonderful courtesy of the American people, the utter absence of restraint or formality and, above all, the amazing energy and enterprise which Americans everywhere import into the varied affairs of life. Nothing must ever disturb our cordial relations with our American cousins, since blood must always remain so much thicker than water.

And finally, how of their prowess in *l'arte de faire l'amour*? Perhaps we should conclude by leaving this question unanswered until I have gained some further experience! That would indeed be a task that I shall willingly undertake – on both sides of the great ocean that divides us!

TO BE CONTINUED

WHITEHALL:
TRAGEDY & FARCE

CLIVE PONTING

THE INSIDE STORY OF HOW WHITEHALL REALLY WORKS

Drawing on fifteen years' experience as a top civil servant in Whitehall, Clive Ponting reveals for the first time the secrets of the closed, amateur, village world of Whitehall and the appalling way in which Britain is really governed.

He shows why the whole system of government is at fault, laying the blame on both the Ministers of the major political parties and the senior Mandarins of the civil service and suggests that only radical changes can produce effective government that might begin to tackle Britain's considerable problems.

In 1985, Clive Ponting provoked a sensational political furore when he was tried and acquitted unanimously at the Old Bailey for passing documents to a Labour MP about the sinking of the *Belgrano*.

And now, in an equally forthright and out-spoken manner, he blows the lid off the all too secret processes of government.

0 7221 6945 0   POLITICS/CURRENT AFFAIRS   £4.95

Also by Clive Ponting in Sphere Books:
THE RIGHT TO KNOW – the Inside Story of the Belgrano Affair

From the bestselling author of SISTERS

Cousins

SUZANNE GOODWIN

Elizabeth Bidwell led an enchanted life on her
uncle's beautiful and rambling estate,
Merriscourt, deep in the heart of the languid
Devonshire countryside. She longed to become
mistress of Merriscourt one day, but her
handsome, charming cousin Peter – who was
destined to inherit the estate – would only flirt and
drop half-promises.

And when distant cousin George Westlock arrives
from India with his stunningly attractive godchild
Sylvia, Elizabeth soon realises that her life and
hopes will change dramatically. For Peter is
captivated by the sylph-like newcomer, as all the
Bidwells are, and Sylvia, a woman who knows
exactly how to get what she wants, is determined
that Peter and Merriscourt will be hers . . .

0 7221 4093 2   GENERAL FICTION   £2.95

Also by Suzanne Goodwin in Sphere Books:
SISTERS

Infidelities

FREDA BRIGHT

The Petersens – the darlings of New York's most glamorous musical and medical circles. Seth, the golden boy of medicine, for whom the Nobel Prize lies within arm's reach. Annie, a woman with the power and determination to realise her potential both as a singer and supportive wife.

Why then, after 10 years of blissful marriage does Annie feel such an agonising, torturing doubt? There's no smear of lipstick, no stray earring, no furtive phonecalls – nothing to confirm her dread. But Annie knows for certain that their world is falling apart . . .

0 7221 1963 1   GENERAL FICTION   £3.99

They played the game . . . with no holds barred

Husbands and Lovers

the sensational new novel from

RUTH HARRIS

Four people living in the fast lane. Four people who thought they had it all . . . and then began to have their doubts.

There was Carlys, with a spectacular career ahead of her, married to the handsome and successful Kirk. But he wasn't enough for her . . .

So she turned to George, every woman's dream who had other lovers besides Carlys; like Jade, the talented fashion designer who'd been burned before but still couldn't help falling for his charms.

So there they were: the Married Woman, the Single Woman, the Husband, the Lover – lost in a tangle of feelings and fantasies wondering if the real thing could ever be found . . .

"A steamy, fast-paced tale . . . you'll be spellbound."
Cosmopolitan

0 7221 4862 3   GENERAL FICTION   £2.95

EVERY WOMAN WANTS HER FANTASY TO COME
TRUE – UNTIL SHE LEARNS THE COST . . .

Private Affairs

The provocative new bestseller – from the author of
POSSESSIONS

JUDITH MICHAEL

The Lovells had a lifestyle of enviable affluence. But for
sixteen years they knew their most treasured dreams had
been put aside in deference to others' needs. Now, before
it was too late, they knew they had to act.

And so Elizabeth and Matt risked everything to buy the
newspaper they'd always longed to own, rekindling both
their youthful ambitions and the passions of their marriage. Yet
in their new-found paradise they met temptations that never
before existed in their small, private world. And the one
thing they needed was fast-slipping out of reach – each
other . . .

GENERAL FICTION   0 7221 6143 3   £4.95

Also by Judith Michael in Sphere Books:
DECEPTIONS
POSSESSIONS

The bittersweet story of a
woman for whom everything wasn't enough . . .

JANET DAILEY

They knew her as 'the girl who had everything'. She
glided through that glamorous international clique of polo
players, country clubs and glittering parties with
effortless ease. There were many women who envied
her . . . until the bombshells hit.

And even when she found the man with whom she felt
she could rebuild her shattered life the problems
weren't over. Because polo wasn't the only thing she had
in common with Raul Buchanan. There were other
women in his life – and one of them was Luz Kincaid's
only daughter . . .

0 7221 2819 3   GENERAL FICTION   £3.50

The explosive saga of power-play and passion
on the international diamond market…

BURT HIRSCHFELD

The top people in the business should have known
better than to take the daughter of a billion-dollar
diamond dynasty at face value. Ellie Foxman was a
woman propelled by the urge to try everything life
had to offer. She thrived on ambition and risk;
accomplishment, reward and acclaim were
her cravings.

To the established order in the world's gem markets
she was a beautiful and very dangerous threat. They
tried to cramp her style. But Ellie Foxman was
determined to go just as far as she wanted. And that
could mean only one thing: to take it all the way…

0 7221 4819 4   GENERAL FICTION   £2.95

Also by Burt Hirschfeld in Sphere Books:
KING OF HEAVEN

A selection of bestsellers from SPHERE

FICTION

AMTRAK WARS VOL. 4	Patrick Tilley	£3.50 ☐
TO SAIL BEYOND THE SUNSET	Robert A. Heinlein	£3.50 ☐
JUBILEE: THE POPPY CHRONICLES 1	Claire Rayner	£3.50 ☐
DAUGHTERS	Suzanne Goodwin	£3.50 ☐
REDCOAT	Bernard Cornwell	£3.50 ☐

FILM AND TV TIE-IN

WILLOW	Wayland Drew	£2.99 ☐
BUSTER	Colin Shindler	£2.99 ☐
COMING TOGETHER	Alexandra Hine	£2.99 ☐
RUN FOR YOUR LIFE	Stuart Collins	£2.99 ☐
BLACK FOREST CLINIC	Peter Heim	£2.99 ☐

NON-FICTION

BURTON: MY BROTHER	Graham Jenkins	£3.50 ☐
BARE-FACED MESSIAH	Russell Miller	£3.99 ☐
THE COCHIN CONNECTION	Alison and Brian Milgate	£3.50 ☐
HOWARD & MASCHLER ON FOOD	Elizabeth Jane Howard and Fay Maschler	£3.99 ☐
FISH	Robyn Wilson	£2.50 ☐

All Sphere books are available at your local bookshop or newsagent, or can be ordered direct from the publisher. Just tick the titles you want and fill in the form below.

Name _____

Address _____

_____

Write to Sphere Books, Cash Sales Department, P.O. Box 11, Falmouth, Cornwall TR10 9EN

Please enclose a cheque or postal order to the value of the cover price plus:

UK: 60p for the first book, 25p for the second book and 15p for each additional book ordered to a maximum charge of £1.90.

OVERSEAS & EIRE: £1.25 for the first book, 75p for the second book and 28p for each subsequent title ordered.

BFPO: 60p for the first book, 25p for the second book plus 15p per copy for the next 7 books, thereafter 9p per book.

Sphere Books reserve the right to show new retail prices on covers which may differ from those previously advertised in the text elsewhere, and to increase postal rates in accordance with the P.O.